THE
WITHERED
MAN

THE
WITHERED
MAN

John Creasey

David McKay Company, Inc.
Ives Washburn, Inc.
New York

THE WITHERED MAN

LIBRARY OF CONGRESS CATALOG CARD NUMBER: 73-81178

MANUFACTURED IN THE UNITED STATES OF AMERICA

ISBN: 0-679-50377-3

I

Rearrangement of Plans

On the day when I first heard of the Withered Man I had
expected so much to be different. For one thing, even Pinky
admitted that I was in need of a rest, and that in itself is
nearly a miracle. Before the war Pinky worked by day and
half the night, and since it started I sometimes wonder if
he ever has more than an hour's uninterrupted sleep. There
is surprising vitality in that plump little body of his, a
startling alertness in the mind behind those bright blue
eyes, which often have the ingenuousness of a child's.

Of course, when I apply cold logic to the problem of
Pinky's hours of sleep I acknowledge that there must be
times when he has uninterrupted nights. But he has defied
so many accepted laws that I don't think I would be surprised if he defied the law of gravity and began walking
across the ceiling of his low, long room in the cottage near
Sloane Square. That cottage is a case in point. What man
in his senses when choosing the headquarters of British
Secret Intelligence (S.1 Branch) would alight on a five-
roomed house in a long terrace and turn the whole of the
upper floor into one big room (plus bathroom) and use the
ground floor for his living quarters? Pinky could have com-
manded a suite of offices in Whitehall but he preferred that
little place near King's Road. I once asked him why.

'Why? You addle-pated young pup,' said Pinky irascibly, 'use what brains the good Lord gave you. I chose

it because no one in their senses would think I really work in it. Most spies have sense.'

There must have been more to it than that, but I have never discovered what.

When I reached the office early in the morning of that fateful day in September I had no thought of asking inconsequential questions. I wanted only to learn why Pinky had to drag me out at half past six on that day of all days. I had gone to sleep, dreamily repeating the questions and answers I had expected to hear and speak on the morrow.

'Wilt thou, Mary Josephine Dell, take this man to thy lawful wedded husband?'

'I will.' It was easy to imagine Mary's low voice, to see her serene face, the grey eyes which had taught me what love meant.

'Wilt thou, Bruce Murdoch, take this woman to thy lawful wedded wife?'

'I will.'

My voice would be husky, of course. I shall never have the calm that Mary has in similar moments. She says that there are times when I seem like a very small and bewildered boy, and strangely enough such a remark does not put me on my dignity.

At Pinky's request, I had recently moved to a small service flat in Park Lane. There I had been disturbed by the bedside telephone, and Pinky's sharp command:

'Get some clothes on, Bruce, and get over here at once.'

There was no denying the command. I dressed hurriedly and without disturbing Percy, my man, and walked to the garage where I kept the Lagonda. Dressing, walking and driving I confounded Pinky and assured myself that even he could do nothing to upset the arrangements for that day. It was the second day of a week's leave which I had been promised regularly since March. During the intervening six months I had been in most European countries, and several in Africa. I had clambered through the smoking

6

ruins of a hotel in Amiens, thankful to be alive and lucky to get a lift in a staff car to the coast. I had been among the last to cross the main bridge near Maastrich over the Albert Canal before the Nazi hordes had thundered in their incredible *blitzkrieg*. I had been in Rotterdam when the parachutists had come down like a swarm of locusts, three in every four dead when they reached the ground. I had been bombed and machine-gunned in an open boat setting off from Flushing. I had seen the sniping from houses and roofs in Louvain during the brief British occupation. I had been in Paris during the first big air-raid, and as luck would have it reached Dover in time for the first assault on the English coast. And I had spent three days and nights in Hamburg when the R.A.F. were bombing the petrol stores and factories.

There had, of course, been many other incidents, and I am so used to bombing that I can hardly remember what the days were like before my baptism. Bombing is hell, but it is surprising how many people escape from hell. That is a sober statement of fact. I once spent an hour arguing with some officers of the Advanced Bombing Squadron in France, and final agreement was reached that the chances of being killed or seriously injured during a night of intense bombing even in a crowded area is no more than one in a thousand. This comforting figure I have often repeated to myself while huddled against a wall and hearing the whine of dropping bombs and the *crump!* of explosions not a hundred yards away.

On all of these occasions I had been working for Pinky, who is more formally known as Sir Robert Holt, O.B.E. Every time I returned to London I found fresh instructions awaiting me, and only three or four times since the affair of the Allaway Plan* had I been able to spend a day with Mary. At least Holt managed to detail her to rather less hazardous appointments. She had been in Rome and Spain,

* Read *Unknown Mission*, by Norman Deane.

7

Portugal, Greece and Turkey. But at last our return journeys had coincided and Pinky had agreed to our having a week off, and the special licence, arrangements with the parson, and everything else necessary for a little ceremony in Chelsea, had been completed.

Imagine, then, my bitterness at Holt's call.

That disappeared very quickly when Gordon, Holt's corpulent and yet self-effacing general factotum, opened the narrow door of the cottage.

'Good morning, sir,' said Gordon as if this were a most normal time for a visit. 'Miss Dell is with him.'

Mary was here! I squeezed past Gordon, no minor task in the narrow hall, and mounted the rickety stairs two at a time. The door of Holt's room was ajar, and his voice was coming through on its alternating current. Pinky was unable to maintain an even level of speech. He squeaked, croaked, or dealt in a deep bass or a high falsetto. I used to think it was affectation, but have since learned that it is due to a minor affliction of the larynx.

'Yes, yes,' Pinky was saying, 'I know he needs a rest, but I can't help it. We can't call our lives our own these days, and b'gad we won't be able to until we've snaffled Adolf. I . . .' Pinky stopped when I opened the door, and his cherubic face switched into a scowl. 'Oh, it's you, is it?' he growled. 'You could have been here five minutes ago. Are you going soft?'

'No, sir. I'm going mad. Today is my wedding day, and . . .'

'Was to have been,' interrupted Pinky, and added gruffly: 'Sorry, Bruce. Can't be helped. I've just been talking to Mary, and she agrees, don't you, my dear?'

Not for the first time I was surprised how fresh Mary could look after only a few hours' sleep. We had not gone to bed until after two the previous night, because of one thing and another. She is nearly as tall as I, and I am close on six feet, but she never gives the impression of being an exceptionally tall woman. She was dressed in a pale grey tailor-made suit with a white silk blouse ruffled at the front, but no hat. I preferred her not to; her dark hair is lovely enough to be seen.

'Hallo, darling,' said Mary, in much the same voice that she would have used for 'I will'.

'Oh, damn,' I said gruffly. 'What is it?'

'That's better,' said Holt. He had been standing by his desk, a small one piled high with papers. Now he stumped round it and sat down, clearing a space for a writing-pad and commencing to scribble without looking at what he was writing.

He is bald but for a few stray grey hairs, and his cranium is as pink as his plump cheeks, which appear so smooth that it is hard to believe that he ever shaves. His blue eyes then were wide and sober.

'Well, Bruce, it's like this. S.1 have been busy, damned busy, in Europe. I don't need to tell you that but you can do with reminding. Others have been looking after things in this country. Others!' snorted the Pink 'Un, and that was not unusual. Among his characteristics is a conviction that no one else does any job thoroughly. 'Well, they've found something that's baulked, stalled, baffled them. So, of course, they come to me. If I could have given you a week or even a few days I would have, but it just couldn't be. He's a damn sight too dangerous.'

'Who is?' I asked sulkily.

'Ah,' said Pinky. He stopped scribbling and screwed up what he had been writing. 'That's the question. Bruce—Mary. Have you ever heard talk of the Withered Man? I don't mean have you overheard a long conversation about him, and don't try to pretend I do! I mean have you heard a rumour, a whisper, even a sigh about him?'

I think Mary was genuinely puzzled. I know I was.

'No,' we answered in unison.

'Hmm,' grunted the Pink 'Un. 'I've asked a dozen people, and get the same answer. They say he's in England.'

'If you've dragged me out of bed and propose cancelling my wedding day because a withered man's in England,' I said with a passable show of indignation, 'I don't think much of it.'

That made Pinky snarl. I knew it would. He is a brilliant man in many ways but I don't think he will ever realise how well Mary and I know him. There is just one way of getting pertinent facts from him without a lot of preamble, and that is to say something which suggests that you are thick-witted.

'You congenital misfit!' roared Pinky. 'I mean *the* Withered Man, the only one of his kind, thank God, the . . .' He sobered down and went on: 'It's like this, Bruce. I've heard whispers, no more than whispers, about a man with one side withered. It's said that he can just walk about with the aid of a stick, but that most of the time he's pushed in a chair. It's also said that he uses an automatic three-wheeler sometimes for getting about. He's been seen in Rotterdam, The Hague, Oslo, Brussels, Amiens and other places. He appears suddenly and disappears as swiftly. There is some-thing amounting to a legend grown about him. Wherever the Withered Man appears, the Nazis strike next. Follow?'

It was not imagination. I went quite cold. I saw Mary start and shiver, only for a split-second but enough for me to know that she felt as I did. It was the way Holt said it, drawing out those words until the *Withered Man* seemed to epitomise all that was foul and evil and obscene in the Nazi organisation.

'There you are,' he said, knowing he'd trapped us. 'I'll give you the proof and all the information I've got in a few minutes, and tell you where you can get more. He's danger-ous. He's *deadly*.'

'But *what* is he?' demanded Mary, helplessly.

'I think that the Withered Man is in control of the Fifth Column in England,' Holt said. 'Get him, smash his or-

ganisation. That is your job. You've *carte blanche*, no
pettifogging restrictions, all the money you want, but—
get the Withered Man!'

2

Old Friends Together

Sir Robert Holt once said that the first essential of a secret
agent was the ability to know when to waste time in thinking and when to act on instinct. Since I started to work
for him, some three years ago, I have often realised the
general truth of that statement. There are more things
necessary for thinking than the capacity. One must have
something to think about, and it frequently happens in the
peculiar work of a spy—and I *am* a spy—that there is
nothing one can profitably ponder.

After Mary and I had interrogated the several French,
Dutch and Belgian refugees who had reported the existence
of the Withered Man, and who claimed to have seen him,
we reached the same conclusion. There was, as yet, nothing
to think about. Holt had given us a virtually impossible
task in searching for a man of whom there were at least
five varying descriptions. The one common denominator
of those reports was that the man was a cripple. He had
been seen in his chair, either being wheeled, or wheeling
himself. He had been seen to walk heavily and cumbersomely with the aid of a heavy ebony stick. Each report
concurred that he walked with great difficulty, drawing his
right leg behind him, and thumping hard with his stick.

He had frightened those who had seen him.

The five men we interviewed, all oldish people, had un-
dergone heavy bombing, ceaseless machine-gunning, and
even artillery fire. They had seen their homes crash about

11

them and become enveloped in flames. They had lost relatives, in some cases their wives and children. They had, in fact, been in just such a frame of mind that makes rumour thrive. They might have been prepared to believe anything.

But there were no generalisations about their fear of the Withered Man. It was coincidence that each of them had lived close to the Town Hall of his home town, and each report agreed that the Withered Man had been wheeled to the door of the Town Hall, and had walked laboriously inside. Parachute troops and advance raiders in possession of the civic buildings in the divers shattered towns had treated him with the utmost respect.

The peculiar thing was, of course, that he had been seen in so many places.

Intelligence might never have heard of the Withered Man until it was too late but for a sharp-witted young man in a junior position at one of the receiving ports for refugees on the South Coast. He had been approached by a white-bearded Dutchman who had told his story in broken English, and said that a Belgian had also seen the man. The official, instead of pooh-poohing the idea, had questioned others and found the five men who later reached Holt, Mary and me. A questionnaire sent out to other receiving ports had brought numerous confirmations of his existence, but Holt had not been called in until one of the witnesses, a French *curé*, had become almost incoherent.

He had seen the man among the refugees!

To that port, which I shall call Hansea, Percy Briggs drove Mary and me soon after ten o'clock on the morning of my rude awakening.

Percy had attached himself to me a long time before I had been assigned to the Pink 'Un, and had become a lesser official in S.1. He is a perky, confident, at times impertinent but always loyal Cockney, and was far more outraged by our change of plans than were we ourselves. It is not easy to grow accustomed to the fact that individual life is unimportant in a time of total war; difficult to accept as a fact that one's own movements, personal happiness and actions are subservient at all times to the war machine. Mary and I had become used to it, and rebelled but a little. Percy, like most Cockneys, would go on rebelling until the end of time.

It was a hot day, with the sun already breaking through the heat-haze of early morning. I was glad the Lagonda was an open car: a closed one would have been stifling. Some 'demolition work' in South London had compelled us to take a long roundabout route, but we were such strangers to the capital that there was a freshness in the proportion of tin-helmeted—'tin' is a colloquialism from the first world-war—air-raid wardens and policemen, many of them armed. There was surprisingly little difference in normal life, except the fact that one saw no children, and virtually no perambulators. Oh, and few women. Work was going on in several places in the street, and there were occasional heaps of rubble where there had been houses before bombs had struck them.

The sun and the autumn mist seemed to give the lie to the brutality of man.

It had been a glorious summer, and we passed many fields where the crop had not only been cut and sheathed, but gathered. Second crops were swaying gently in the wind in some fields, and twice we passed parties of convalescent soldiers working at the harvest. Except for these, the labourers in the fields were women or old men, and children were far more frequent.

An Automobile Association scout with a rifle slung over his shoulder stopped us outside Winchester, and demanded to see our identity cards. He saluted smartly when he saw our passes.

'Good luck, sir!'

'Good luck to you,' I said, while Percy fumed at the wheel. 'All right, Briggs.'

I always call Percy by his surname when I feel that he is in need of rebuke, and he hunched his shoulders more over the wheel and let the Lagonda touch seventy. Nearing Southampton we saw military patrols and once or twice aircraft zoomed over the fields on either side. If there was anything surprising in what we saw it was the normalcy that appeared to abound everywhere. England fitted in to the conditions of total war with a deceptive indifference.

We were made to take a long route past Southampton, and reached Hansea just after midday. Before we reached the refugee quay we were questioned three times and had to produce our passes. Once through, and waiting for the intelligent official who had started this chase, Mary said with sudden vehemence:

'Oh, God! Why does it *have* to be?'

'If God made the men,' I said mildly, 'the men made the fools of themselves. Or beasts, if you prefer it.'

It was easy to see what had disturbed her. By then I had become hardened to refugees, and knew that the crowds inside the stockades near the quay and waiting for boats, trains or coaches to take them to their camps or billets were comparatively well off. Comparatively, I mean, when considering their plight of a few weeks or a few months before. How often I had been in a car driving through the masses of old men, women and children, seeing their cheeks drawn with pain, anxiety and hunger, a few pitiful parcels of belongings on their backs, or in hand-carts, or on cycles piled so high that no two wheels were likely to stand the strain. Some had, but many had fallen by the wayside, and were now rotting in ditches and hedges. I had seen whole columns of the tragic hosts rush terror-stricken for nearly non-existent cover at the sound of an approaching 'plane.

I do not know whether the story of that refugee host will ever be told in full. If it is it will be the story of the grimmest pilgrimage of sorrow ever heard.

Yet these people were happy. Children were playing

and shouting, women gossiping or quarrelling, old men sitting and wagging their beards. Miraculously, they were clean.

A youthful man, looking no more than nineteen or twenty, came up to us. His fair hair was untidy, and there was a line of moisture on the down of his upper lip. His collar was awry, and the knot of his tie close to his ear. He ran his fingers through his hair and straightened the tie, with a rueful:

'One of the kids jumped on my back, I'm afraid. What was it I asked you to come to see me about?'

'You were going to introduce us to a certain *curé*,' I said gravely.

The blue eyes widened.

'Oh, on *that* business. Sorry, but I've a thousand-and-one things on my hands and it gets rather confusing. Father André is conducting a service in one of the huts. Confessional, or something. I'm not R.C., but if ever a man *radiates* goodness it is he. I say,' added the young man with a sudden eagerness, 'do you think there's anything in this Withered Man business?'

'It seems possible,' I said.

'I'd like to join in the hunt for him,' the other said. 'I've a dicky heart, you know. That's why I'm a non-combatant. But there are thousands of people who could do this job, and I often wish I could do something more active.'

'May we have your name?' Mary asked.

'Denyer,' said the youth briefly. 'Mark Denyer. You'll have to push your way through the crowd, I'm afraid.'

The crowd, in fact, made a lane for us. Denyer was greeted warmly on all sides, more especially by the children.

As we reached a corrugated iron shed half a dozen people came out, and Denyer said something in French to one of them. I was surprised at his control of the language and the fact that he had no difficulty in following the *patois*

15

of a man I identified as a peasant from Alsace or Lorraine. The *curé*, it seemed, was now with a young woman refugee who had made a special request to see him alone. She had lost her husband, and she was heartbroken. M'sieu Denyer could perhaps let priest and young widow have a few minutes alone? Denyer looked at me.

Well, a few minutes made no difference. We might easily have been delayed that long on the road. I nodded, and Denyer excused himself. There was a free fight going on between half a dozen children, and his arrival settled it in a few minutes. A woman called, and I saw him talking earnestly to her, but did not worry long about Denyer, for Mary gripped my arm.

'Bruce—there's Mick and Ted!'

'*What!*' I said, and followed the direction of her gaze.

At first I could hardly believe my eyes. There, amongst the crowds of refugees, were Mick Fuller and Ted Angell, agents of S.1 with whom Mary and I have always worked. We had no idea they were detailed to this job. Ted Angell, tall and angular, wearing four days' growth of stubble, scruffy and dressed in an old boiler suit and a red beret, shuffled towards us. In deliberate undertones he demanded:

'What the devil are *you* doing here? And if you must come, why don't you look a little less like tailors' dummies? And weren't you going to be married today?'

'Never mind that,' said Mary. 'What are you doing, Ted?'

'Mixing with the mob,' said Ted, casting his eyes towards the ground. He had snatched his beret off, and appeared as a supplicant before us. No one watching would dream that the last time we had met he had been in evening dress, as debonair a man-about-town as there was in London. 'There were some suspects in a boatload starting off from Boulogne,' he went on, 'and Pinky put us with them.'

'Have you heard of the Withered Man?' I asked.

'Yes,' said Ted, but he quickly dashed what hopes I

16

had from that admission. 'We had a *billet-doux* from Pinky not half an hour ago, telling us to keep our ears open for mention of him. But that's all.'

'Did Pinky give you any other instructions?'

Ted's eyes sparkled, although he was twisting his beret in his large hands.

'He said we'd be working with you two soon, and I'm not going to grumble about that. Send any word through by Denyer—he knows we're not the usual run of refugees. A nice lad that.' He nodded his head two or three times in quick succession, backed away and then turned to join Mick Fuller, a shorter, broader man who was dressed in an appalling cycling suit that might have come from the late Victorian era.

We looked towards the shed that the *curé* had turned into a church, and saw the door open. A girl, she was little more, came out. She had her eyes cast towards the ground and her shoulders were bowed. She wore a red blouse and a yellow—yes, yellow—skirt, and her absurdly high-heeled shoes were badly worn. They made her hobble. It was at her head that we looked most, however, for she was wearing a small black hat with a long veil that dropped to her waist. The mourning weeds were incongruous against the brightness of the other part of her ensemble.

Mary said: 'Poor creature.'

'Yes,' I admitted. 'But she's better off here than in France or Belgium, I suppose. I will say she's a looker!'

'And on our wedding day,' Mary said in mock reproach.

The girl was exceptionally good-looking. I had seen her profile for a moment as she had raised her head when a woman had approached her. The profile made me want to see her full-face. It had line and beauty and dignity, and she shook her head and hurried past the woman who had intercepted her.

Denyer appeared, hot but unruffled.

'I expect it's all clear,' he said. 'We'll get inside, and

then when I've introduced you I'll shove off. Er—the *curé's* an awfully decent old stick,' he added awkwardly. 'You won't grill him or anything like that, will you?'

'My dear man,' I said, 'we want a description and details of the Withered Man, and nothing more.'

Denyer nodded and pushed open the door. The little hut was hot but shadowy. Through a small window at the far end a shaft of sunlight shone on to a small, home-made altar on which fifty or sixty candles were burning, some of them almost burnt out. In front of the alter the *curé* was kneeling, his head bowed in his hands.

'Father André,' called Denyer softly.

There was silence.

'Father!' Denyer raised his voice, but there was still no movement.

The youngster stepped closer, but I was before him, pushing him roughly aside in sudden alarm. I reached the *curé* with my heart hammering and my hand unsteady, but those symptoms went completely when I saw that I was right.

For plunged into the *curé's* back was a knife. The hilt protruded several inches, and the blade had almost certainly reached the heart.

3
The Yellow Skirt

I turned sharply from the murdered priest, and said to Denyer:

'Go outside and tell the two men who received a special message this morning to come here at once. Then get a doctor. If Father André's alive and regains consciousness, make a note of all he can tell you. Is that clear?'

Denyer took it well, although even in the gloom of that little sanctuary which had been so violently maltreated I could see that his face was chalk white.

'Yes,' he said, and hurried to the door.

'And have some people look for the woman who just left here,' I called.

Denyer left the shed a few seconds before Mary and I. Outside, the bright sunshine made us blink, but we kept moving. Two armed guards at the narrow doorway in the barbed wire fence making the stockade, stiffened as we approached.

'Has anyone left within the last five minutes?' I demanded.

'No, sir.'

'Get word to the other gates,' I said. 'Have them closed immediately. Never mind about authority, you can't do any harm in obeying that!'

I thought the man might argue, but he lifted a field telephone behind him, and I heard him say:

'Requested that all gates are closed at once. Has anyone left in the last few minutes?'

The telephone crackled before the receiver was replaced.

'A coach has just gone out, sir,' said the sentry.

I could see the parking places for coaches, about two hundred yards away, and rushed towards it, pushing roughly past some refugees, and in my urgency I sent a woman off her balance. Her Flemish curses echoed in my ears, with several oaths from men who had seen the incident.

Mary was just behind me, and when I glanced behind I saw that Ted and Mick were on the way.

The Lagonda, and Percy Briggs, were on the other side of the quay, and there was no hope of help from them. When I reached the main gates, they were guarded by half a dozen men with fixed bayonets, and two coach-loads of refugees were standing with the engines turning over.

'I'll look for her,' Mary said. 'You arrange for a car.'

I was lucky. A young lieutenant was approaching, probably attracted by my urgency. I showed my identity card, and he was on his toes in a trice.

'What can I do, sir?'

'Get me a car,' I said, 'and have the coach which has just gone out stopped on the road. Was it equipped with radio?'

'I doubt it.'

'Telephone as far ahead as you can,' I said, and I saw a green-grey camouflaged Talbot on the other side of the gate. 'May I use that bus?'

'Yes, that's all right. I came in it.' He gave an order to the guards and the gates were opened. Mary said urgently:

'She's not here. Don't forget Ted and Mick.'

They were hurrying up, but a sentry was going towards them and was likely to stop them getting out. I shouted to the lieutenant, and he yelled an order in a voice so loud that even the sentry started. The four of us rushed towards the Talbot. Not until I was at the wheel did I realise that I did not know what road out of Hansea the coach had taken. I had assumed that the woman in the yellow skirt was on the coach, and certainly she had been walking in the direction of the car park.

The lieutenant saved the day. He had sent a coach driver after us, and the man jumped to the running board.

'I'll guide you through the town, sir.'

'Right.' I let in the clutch, and got away to a good start. 'Where's the coach going?'

'To a New Forest village, sir, or a camp nearby.'

'Good,' I said. 'Did you see the passengers loading?'

'Yes, sir.'

I had no time to look at the driver, who was clinging to the door at my side and holding the windscreen with one hand. For the second time that day I blessed the fact that

I was in an open car. The roads were clear, and I did not worry about the speed limit.

We were travelling at forty miles an hour, and I had to shout.

'Did you see a woman in a yellow skirt?'

'And a red blouse!' called Mary.

'A young woman,' I yelled.

The coach driver was gasping for breath, and it was seconds before he could answer. Then he crouched low behind the windscreen, so that the onrush of wind did not send the words back into his throat.

'Ye-es! She got on—last minnit!'

'Right,' I said.

My foot went down so heavily on the accelerator that the coach driver was jolted inches into the air. He hung on as if used to riding wild, and shouted from time to time:

'First left—next right—mind them traffic lights—*left again.*' He was supremely confident, swaying outwards when we swung left, hugging the side of the car when we went right. Soon we were out of the main part of the town, and going through the wide roads of the suburbs. I could remember only the yellow-skirted woman with the lovely profile, and the kneeling *curé* with the knife in his back.

On the open road we were soon touching sixty. The commonland of the New Forest was on either side of us, and we could see the road for a mile or more ahead. As we breasted a rise, I saw the coach ahead of us. It was disappearing into an avenue of trees, and I felt a surge of excitement: we would be up with it in a few minutes.

'Careful here!' yelled the coach man.

I saw what he meant, but would have missed it until too late but for the shout. There was a tiny hump-backed bridge over a stream and if I had crossed it at sixty the guide must have been dislodged, and badly injured. The Talbot's brakes squealed as I slowed down, and I half expected the man to call it a day and jump off. The idea did not seem to occur to him.

Once over the bridge I went all out.

Even at the high speed that avenue of trees seemed a long time coming, and I scowled when I saw that the road turned ahead of me once I was under the trees, and the coach was still out of sight. And then, taking the bend wider than I should, I found myself faced with the imminence of a disaster which could have been fatal to us all.

The coach was stopped, and drawn across the road!

My tyres were screaming on the bend already, and as I jammed on foot and hand brakes I felt a sickening surge in the pit of my stomach. It was impossible to avoid a crash. I could see the dozens of refugees inside backing away, fear on every face. I even heard a woman scream. I kept my foot down hard, and my teeth were biting so fiercely against each other that my jaws ached.

Then came the crash.

Just before I hit the side of the coach the Talbot had jolted with the extra pressure of the brakes, but I was driving at fully twenty miles an hour when the collision happened. There was a breaking of glass, and more shouting and screaming from the running-board. My body was lifted out of the driving seat, and I felt the steering wheel thud against my stomach. By great good luck my head went higher than the windscreen, which caught me across the top of the chest.

The grinding din of the radiator against the side of the coach was ugly, but the Talbot was at a standstill and I was still alive. I managed to turn my head and look at Mary. She was already on her feet, and trying to open her door. By then Mick Fuller had jumped from the back, so he was all right. He jerked open Mary's door, while in my ear came Ted Angell's anxious voice.

'Are you all right, Bruce?'

'Damn silly—thing to—ask,' I gasped.

22

Ted grinned and opened my door, and with his help I reached the road.

Afterwards, I learned that the driver of the coach had jumped down to stop traffic coming from the other direction, and that my guide—who had escaped with only a shaking—hurried to stop anything else coming round the corner. Mary and Mick reached the coach, and began to look over the scared passengers, less concerned with any possible injuries than with finding the woman in the yellow skirt.

Ted meanwhile forced a spot of whisky into my mouth. I swallowed, believing that I would bring it up again in one movement, but I was wrong. It went down and stayed down, and a second dose steadied me amazingly. Mary had gone ahead and was talking to the driver of the damaged coach. As I drew up I heard him say:

'I never would've thought it. She didn't look that kind at all, Miss.'

As the coach driver had turned the corner, it proved, one of the passengers behind him—the girl—had drawn a revolver. Refugees and driver alike had been scared. The girl, dressed in black, yellow and red, had forced the driver to draw the coach across the road, and while he had been doing that a man from a private car drawn up ahead had pulled open the coach door.

The girl had jumped down.

At that point in the man's story I broke in.

'Can you describe the man, driver?'

'Well, sir, 'e was a youngish feller. I didn't get a good look at 'im, mind you. 'Ad a sing-song voice, I can say that. "Hur-*ree*, El-*sa*," 'e said.'

'Elsa.' I rolled the name over my tongue, for it was the nearest approach to direct information I had. I felt sick with disappointment and a sense of failure, as well as physically. It was no use assuring myself that I had not been

23

able to prevent what had happened: it was my job to prevent it, and there was no room for excuses.

Then suddenly I saw a gleam of hope.

Approaching at a good speed, brakes already squealing, was a small Ford. As it slowed down I said sharply to the coach driver:

'What car did she get away in?'

'An Austin 12, sir.'

'Colour?'

'Black, or it might'a been a very dark blue.'

'Thanks,' I said. 'Ask that fellow to turn,' I said to Mary. 'What's the road like ahead, driver?'

The coach driver scratched his head.

'There ain't a turn for two or three miles, and then there's a lot of curves and a lot of crossroads.'

By then Mick and Ted had joined us—Ted had slipped back for Mick—and the driver of the Ford proved not only amenable but eager to help. We crowded in, Mary, myself and Mick in the back and Ted next to the driver. The overloaded small car made a fair speed. In three or four minutes we were in sight of the crossroads and branch-turnings which the coach driver had mentioned.

There was a roughly prepared barricade right in front of us, and an A.A. man and an army private were guarding it. As we slowed down the private hurried up, with the sun glistening on his bared bayonet.

'Identity cards, please,' he said.

I started to take my pass out, and doing so, glanced towards a road which forked left. I went rigid and stared intently.

For hanging on the leafy branches of a hawthorn hedge was a skirt—the skirt, I felt sure, of the bright yellow which the escaped 'refugee' had worn.

4

Ernst

There is a lot to be said for routine and the strict obedience
to orders, but the lot of a British agent working in his own
country is not a happy one. I wanted speed, but this guard
had to be satisfied of all our credentials.

Mary had shown her pass, and:

'Why is this barricade necessary, Sergeant?'

That little trick worked. The youngster was flattered by
the 'sergeant', and perhaps Mary's good looks helped.

'I don't really know, miss, but orders to put it up come
from Hansea not five minutes ago.'

'That's quick work,' I said. 'I gave the orders. Where
were you before the order came?'

'Just guarding the crossroads, sir.'

It was hard to believe but true that all the crossroads in
England were guarded against parachutists, either by regu-
lars or the Volunteer Defence Corps, but I did not think
about it then.

'Did you see a black Austin 12?'

'Can't say I did, sir.' The private was satisfied with the
credentials, and I said to the driver:

'Take that left-hand fork, please, and tread on it. Sergeant'—I had to bellow this, since we were already on the
road—'take that yellow thing down and save it for me!
And send word for all Austin 12s to be stopped.'

The man stared, but the A.A. scout went across to the
yellow skirt. Craning my neck, I could see that he was un-
hooking it from the hedge with the aid of his rifle.

A bend in the road took them out of sight.

The driver of the Ford, a middle-aged man who had
not spoken except to agree to our proposal, at last asked

25

what it was all about. Some kind of explanation was owed
to him, and I said:

'We're looking for a Fifth Columnist who came over
with some refugees and escaped from Hansea.'

'Are you, by Jove!' I could not see the driver's face,
but the little car went faster, and he settled more steadily
over the wheel. All the same, I longed for the Talbot; and
even more for Percy Briggs and the Lagonda.

We could see for miles on either side, and although we
occasionally passed narrow by-roads leading into the forest
I decided to take a chance that our quarry had turned
neither right nor left. I had time to think more about the
whole situation, but no time for discussing it even had I
wanted to with the strange driver in earshot. It was hot,
and the back of the car was crammed with sticky people.
Even when Mary wriggled on to my knee, leaving more
room for Mick, we were tightly wedged.

The road began to wind downwards, and no longer could
we see the moorland on either side of us. Steep banks rose
above us and we were forced to travel at crawling speed.
There was a nasty moment when the driver decided he
could make up a mile or so, and as he eased on the accelerator down a steep hill, a crow flew right across the windscreen. It struck one side with a dull thud and the driver
momentarily lost control of the wheel. Ted shot out his
hand and grabbed at the brake. The car skidded but missed
the bank, and the driver apologised and went straight on.

Then we reached some crossroads, where a man in the
uniform of the L.D.V. sitting in a sentry-box and smoking,
hastily stubbed the cigarette out when we slowed down.

I called: 'We're looking for an Austin 12. Has one
passed?'

'What colour would it be?' The man spoke in the slow
voice of a Hampshire man.

'Black or cobalt blue.'

'Well, there *was* one took the Burley Road about five minutes ago.'

My heart leapt.

'How many people in it?'

'Three,' said the L.D.V. man thoughtfully. 'Three, that's right. A lady and two gentl'men. Smiled to me as they passed, she did.'

The Ford driver was already turning right. The road was hilly and often deep between high banks. We could not see more than fifty or sixty yards at any time until we reached Burley village. I know the New Forest fairly well, and of all the tiny villages in it I think Burley takes a lot of beating for picturesqueness.

A steel-helmeted policeman was in the centre of the crossroads, and two V.D.C. men were interrogating the drivers of three cars pulled up in front of me.

'Get alongside the front one,' I said.

The driver obeyed, and the policeman shouted as we appeared to be trying to get straight past. A rifle was levelled from a Defence Corps volunteer, but I showed my pass as we screeched to a standstill.

'We're after an Austin 12,' I said.

'Oh, *you're* after it.' The man's face cleared. 'We was told someone was coming. One passed us on the Ringwood road five minutes ago, sir, just afore the message came.'

We were no more than five minutes behind our quarry —the woman Elsa who, presumably, had killed the *curé*. Five minutes was between us and a capture which might prove of considerable importance, might even take us to the Withered Man.

And then, turning a sharp bend, we found our car!

It was drawn into the side of the road, but the thing that proved its identity was the scarlet blouse draped over one wheel. The oddness of that struck me then, and for the first time made me suspicious of the yellow skirt which had been high in the hedge some miles back.

The car was a black Austin.

Our driver slowed down.

'No, go on!' cried Mary. She was sitting on me so that I could not get a clear view of the road. Craning my neck, I saw what had attracted her attention. Running towards a patch of trees and bushes some half a mile from the road was a man dressed in black. He was not looking behind him, and his elbows were tucked well into his sides.

The driver did not need telling what to do.

He swung the wheel towards the man and we bumped and rattled over the uneven gorse and heathland. We gained only slowly, and it looked as if our quarry would reach the trees first. I said to Ted:

'Take a pot at him, now.'

Ted drew an automatic from his blouse and squeezed himself through the window. In that position it was difficult to take a careful aim, and the bumping of the car did not help, but as Ted fired and the sharp *crack!* of the first bullet came with the flash of bluish flame, I saw a spurt of dust kick up just in front of the man. It startled him, for he hesitated. The next bullet went wider yet the effect was even better. The man ahead stopped running, and turned round. His hands went skywards, and he advanced slowly towards us.

I saw a dark-haired man with a wisp of dark moustache, side-whiskers, and a sallow face from which two remarkably large and expressive eyes shone. He showed no signs of fear except that he was still holding his arms above his head.

'Keep him covered,' said I.

One of the lessons of the war has been to find that there is nothing that a Nazi will not do. Had Ted put his gun away I think Ernst—for we learned that was his name— would have seized the chance to shoot at us, for he was carrying two automatics.

We stopped twenty yards from him. Mary squeezed out,

and I followed her. Ted still leaned from the window with his gun trained. Mick followed Mary and me, and I was in no mood for wasting time.

'Turn round,' I said sharply, and Ernst grinned an unpleasant gloating grin, and obeyed. I ran my hands about his body quickly, finding an automatic in a shoulder holster, and another in his coat pocket. I resisted a temptation to kick his rear, and swung him round. Even that treatment did not knock the grin off his face.

I said: 'Where are the others?'

'Would you not like to know that?' demanded Ernst, and I knew that he was the man who had opened the door of the coach, for his voice was a sing-song more to be expected from an Italian, Spaniard or Frenchman than a German.

'Yes,' I said, 'and I will, if you know it.'

Ernst showed his teeth, which were pointed and yellow.

'I do not know,' he said. 'I am Hans Ernst, and I am a prisoner of yours. I rely on you to take me to the proper au-thorities.' His English was good, but he split some words into more than syllables, as if trying to remember their pronunciation. 'I was with the others who took a dif-fer-ent car and I come away in this one to lead you as-tray.'

I had suspected it too late, of course.

When I had seen the red blouse draped over the wheel, and remembered the yellow skirt, I knew that I had fallen for an obvious trick, and yet for some reason I did not blame myself as much as I had over the earlier failure. I suppose that was because in Ernst I had a prisoner.

'I see,' I said, and deliberately I smiled. It was not a pleasant expression and it wiped the grin off Ernst's lips. 'You've made one mistake,' I went on. 'You were quite wrong about being taken to the proper authorities. Have you ever heard the story about the man being shot while trying to escape?'

As I spoke I handled one of his own guns carelessly, and I saw his sallow face go sallower, and I knew that he was very frightened.

5

Says Percy

Some of you, a very few, may have been struck across the face with a rubber truncheon wielded by a Storm-trooper or an S.S. man. If you have, you will know that he does not strike lightly. Some months before the war began I was in Germany, and had my jaw dislocated by this means. I have also been 'concentrated', and there is nothing nice about that. I was lucky in getting out of Germany, for had it been suspected that I was an English agent and not just a Social Democrat I would have been liquidated very quickly. Happily, I have a fair command of my native Scots, although I have been bred in England, and a Scotsman finds it easier to get the German guttural over successfully. That was the reason that Pinky so often selected me for hazardous ventures in Berlin, Hamburg, and Cologne, among other places, and is a reason for my intense hatred of the individual Nazi.

Hans Ernst was a Nazi.

I cannot help it if I am told that two wrongs never make a right, that brutality need not breed brutality, that hatred is an unchristian emotion, and that a German is a man just as I am. To such generalisations I do not turn a deaf ear: I deliver an attack as vehement as I have at my command. I have met good Germans—even a sporting Prussian. I know the kindly, slow-thinking Bavarian would not deliberately hurt a fly unless dragooned by his organisers. There is many a plump and laughing Frau in the

Black Forest whom I remember with pleasure, many a friendly talk in a beer-garden which I recall, with regret that the days of fraternising are over for the time being. But I have never yet been brought into contact with *any* example of a Nazi who is not a complete brute.

I have known men as good as the next before the poison of the brown shirt propaganda befouled their very souls.

All this is necessary to show you my reaction towards the scared Hans Ernst.

All of the others were watching Ernst. The owner of the Ford had a fixed smile on his face, and was nervous. He was a corpulent man with a florid face and the blue-veined nose of the heavy drinker.

I said: 'Ted, find a clearing in that copse where we can deal with this fellow. You needn't stay, Mary.' I ignored Ernst, but out of the corner of my eye could see his lips working. 'Will you give me your name and address,' I said to the Ford driver. 'I'll see that you get compensation for loss of time, and petrol to make up for what you've used with us.'

'I don't want compensation,' said the man quickly, and he was eyeing Ernst almost as if he were to be the 'victim'. 'But the petrol *would* be useful. Here's my card.' I accepted the slip of pasteboard, and he went on: 'But won't you need me again?'

'I'll get you to telephone to a garage for a larger car to come out here,' I said.

But that suggestion was nearly stillborn.

Ted had disappeared into the copse of trees, and Mick was lighting a pipe. He jumped when the match flared and singed his stubble—his hair grows very quickly. Mary had walked a few yards away from me, when she exclaimed:

'There's Percy!'

I stared, suddenly hopeful.

It was true. Percy, at the wheel of the Lagonda, was pulling up at the side of the road. He would not drive the car onto the rough except under orders. He came hurrying over, a chunky figure in an obtrusively loud check coat. He wears a chauffeur's uniform only under the strictest protest unless we are in town.

He had been in the open air so much of recent months that his ugly face was browned to an attractive shade of medium oak, and his eyes were brighter and bluer because of it. His face is uneven, because his broken nose is pushed to one side, and he can twist his lips to look really villainous. He did then.

' 'Ere—where the 'ell 'ave you bin?' he demanded before he was with us. 'What do you mean by going orf without me?'

Percy is like that—truculent to a point of insolence at times. But it needs only a sharp word to deal with him.

'That's enough,' I said. 'I'll deal with you later. I can't thank you enough, Mr. . . .' I consulted the card. 'Ebbley, I really can't. I won't need a car now, but I'll see you get a generous supply of petrol coupons.'

'Oh, *that* will be wonderful,' said Ebbley.

He climbed into the Ford, but before he drove off I saw him put a flask to his lips and take a long drink. I turned to Ernst.

'Now,' I said, 'I'll deal with you.'

I swung him round and gave him a push so violent that he stumbled and nearly fell. Ted had come out of the copse, and was beckoning. Ernst did not wait for another shove, but hurried towards Ted. Percy stared at me wide-eyed, and deliberately I winked. Percy caught on in a flash, and began a violent verbal attack on all things Nazi, using a bastard English-cum-French-cum-German and making his threats sound more blood-curdling than they were. By the time we reached the little clearing which Ted had located Ernst was trembling violently. Only a man who had watched others tortured and delighted in it, quakes like that at the thought of it happening to him.

32

In the clearing, a pleasant, grass-clad spot sheltered from the heat of the sun and humming with a myriad tiny insects and occupied at one corner by a rabbit so startled that it had not turned to run, I barked:

'That's far enough. Turn round.'

Ernst obeyed promptly.

'I would say . . .' he began in that sing-song voice, but I cut him short with a bellow:

'Talk to answer questions, that's all! Who is Elsa?'

If it were possible his fear grew even more craven. I thought for a moment that he was going on his knees, but he kept upright somehow.

'She—she is a friend of me, Herr . . .'

'Why did she kill the priest?'

'She—she killed no one!' gasped Ernst, and I could believe he was unaware of what had happened. 'She was with the refugees, yes, I was waiting in the car, with a radio. I had a word from her, to wait for her on the road, to make arrangements to help her escape! That is all, I swear it is all! I make them, I do them well and then she goes on to London in one car, I take you away from her the way I said. I know of nothing she did!'

'Don't lie to me!' I barked, but I was afraid he was telling the truth as far as he knew it. 'What car is she in?'

'It was a Morris, a Morris 10.'

'Will she change it *en route*?'

'I do not know,' gasped Ernst. 'Me, I was to take care of her until Romsey, that was all. Beyond that, others will arrange for her to be safe.'

This opened up a variety of possibilities, which were mostly depressing. Of course, I knew there were Fifth Columnists in England. I have been among the many who have seen them at work in other countries before invasions, and I had continually pleaded with Holt to urge Government action here. That, of course, was before the changeover in May after that astonishing debate on Nor-

33

way, when all predictions of 'no challenge to the Government' were proved baseless. I had never admired the retiring Prime Minister except as a gentleman, but I respected him as a very gallant loser when he resigned on the day of the onslaught on the Low Countries, and thus proved again that Great Britain is the most incalculable country.

But I felt sick at this assurance of a regional organisation to protect Elsa. Here was a 'refugee' who could stick a knife in the back of a praying priest and within ten minutes be on the way to comparative safety in an enemy country.

I said: 'What is her name?'

'El . . .' He hesitated. 'Elsa Bruenning.'

'Who else was with her in the car?'

And then I saw Ernst's self-control go completely, which was a remarkable fact. Even he must have seen by then that I was not likely to proceed with the threats which I had made by inference, and Percy by word of mouth. He must have sensed that the situation was easier for him, and he had the satisfaction of knowing that Elsa was safe for the time being. Yet at that innocent-seeming question his control broke.

Mary had, after all, followed me, and I could see her staring at Ernst as though at a ghost. Ted Angell had stopped grinning behind the prisoner's back, and Percy swallowed an imaginary lump in his throat.

All this is gospel truth, *and yet the Withered Man had not been mentioned*.

I knew as I saw the man's face go ashen and his hands tremble, that Elsa had been with the Withered Man. I cannot explain that knowledge, and nothing dragged a word of admission from Ernst. He sobbed as Percy and Ted dragged him up from his knees, and Percy punched at his face, missing deliberately except with one light blow on the nose. He gasped out a constant stream of protestations that he did not know the man's name, he did not know anything about him. Then out of the blue Mary said:

'So it was the Withered Man, Ernst.'

Ernst turned towards her, his mouth opening and closing until he gasped the words which were difficult to hear.

'So—you know. *Mein Gott,* you *do* know. Elsa was right!'

And then that peculiar representative of the Nazi Fifth Column fainted.

. . . . . ,

In spite of numerous delays on the road, mostly due to barricades put up hastily and in front of which there were long streams of cars whose drivers were being questioned, Percy made the run from Ringwood to London in two and a half hours. It was clear from the way in which he crashed his gears that he remained in a bad temper. I was not concerned. I have grown used to Percy, and would not be without him for a fortune.

My pass earned us priority, although many a dubious look was cast towards Mick and Ted. Seeing that the patrols were on the watch for an escaped 'refugee' this was not surprising.

Ernst, once round, kept silent throughout the journey.

I was taking no chances and had handcuffed him—there was usually a pair of handcuffs in the Lagonda. To reduce the margin of error to a minimum, Mary and I left the car at Victoria, and went to Sloane Square by taxi. Percy and the others were to drive on to an apartment near Regent's Park, which served as an unofficial receiving office for gentlemen of Ernst's persuasion. The Pink 'Un had not yet returned, and Gordon told me that he was at Whitehall. I busied myself with several minor items, including an order to send a generous supply of petrol coupons to Ebbley.

'And I've half a mind to send him a case of Johnnie Walker,' I said to Mary.

'At sixteen shillings a bottle you can keep it as half a mind,' retorted Mary.

'I,' said I, 'am the Scotsman of this party.'

Neither of us was in the mood of repartee, however. The way in which that kneeling *curé* floated in and out of my mind was nightmarish. Mary and I would have started a discussion on it had Pinky not arrived, carrying with him a neat brown paper parcel. He stumped across to his desk, sat down and scribbled a few notes, then pushed his pad aside and looked up. Pinky finds it easier to remember things he has once written down. His mind must be like a mountainous pile of shorthand notebooks.

'Well,' he said, 'I've heard about André. Word reached me from the refugee fellow.'

'Denyer,' I said. I felt miserable and useless. After all, that priest had been murdered within fifty yards of me. 'I'm desperately sorry about it, sir. It's damnable to think we might have found something really conclusive about the Withered Man if I'd insisted on seeing the *curé* immediately.'

Holt didn't mince words.

'It was bad, yes. You ought to know by now that nothing —*nothing*—must delay you when you're working. Had that woman been genuine she could have had her private audience with André afterwards, whereas your business couldn't wait.'

'She might have found some other way of killing him,' Mary said. She never lets Holt get away with a thing if she can prevent it.

'Oh, all right, all right,' Holt growled. 'It's happened and it can't be helped. Now let me have the whole story.'

In a little more than ten minutes Holt had all the essentials. He kept plucking at his flabby chin and squinting down at his pad from time to time, when he would scribble furiously. When I finished, he asked:

'Well, what do you make of it?'

'It seems,' I began cautiously, 'as if the *curé* could tell me something, and the woman Bruenning meant to make sure that he did not. She must have learned who I was after.'

'Yes,' said Holt, and his scowl grew darker. 'Yes. She must have done. On the other hand she couldn't possibly have done.' I let this remarkable statement pass as he went on: 'Only you two and I knew about it. Unless you'd told Briggs.'

'No,' I said.

'There you are.' Holt banged his fist on the desk. 'She couldn't have known. But she did know that the *curé* had information about the Withered Man. She probably heard you asking young what's-his-name for him. That made her act. But she was all set to get out of the camp quickly. Ernst was waiting ten miles away to put you off the track. It's clever and it's thorough. She would be picked up by another car, probably two or three more before she arrived in London. She may have changed her clothes half a dozen times. Gordon 'phoned me after you'd been through, and I've had the roads watched for a man who might be considered withered. But,' he added with a growl, 'you can't tell what a man's like when he's sitting in a car.'

'No,' I said. 'And this wheel-chair business might be a blind.'

Holt blinked.

'Yes. Don't know why, Bruce, but I've taken it for granted that our man is really crippled. Well! It's reasonable to assume that he's somewhere near London, and the woman is with him. We've two people to look for instead of one. Did you get a fuller description of the woman?'

'No,' I said. 'We didn't have much time.'

'Hmm.' Pinky lifted up the telephone, and was connected with his main office—perhaps I should say his staff office —in Whitehall. He said: 'There's a man down at the Hansea Refugee Reception Station. Denby, Denyer or something. I want him at the office, quick. Have him bring any photographs available of the woman who escaped this morning. Got that? Well, get on with it, get on with it, my gel!' roared Pinky, and banged down the receiver. Then he grinned at Mary and me. 'I get more and more bad-tempered as the days go by, don't I? Not surprising when I'm surrounded with dunderheads like you!' He glared. 'Where's Ernst?'

'At the flat,' I said.

'Is he likely to talk?'

'I don't think so,' I said.

'I don't think he knows much,' Mary put in.

'All right,' said Pinky. 'Keep him at the flat. I'll have him questioned from time to time.'

Pinky is one of the men who has really adjusted to the new conditions of war thoroughly. There have been numerous men, in Ernst's position, who have been questioned and even third-degreed at the Regent's Park flat until they have become shivering relics of what they were.

The flat, of course, is unofficial.

'And now,' said Pinky, 'we've got to look for the man and woman. I wonder if this will help?' he added unexpectedly, and carefully untied the knot of the parcel he had brought in, rolling the string up and putting it in a drawer. I saw the patch of yellow inside the brown paper. A moment later Pinky drew out the yellow skirt which I had last seen draped on a Hampshire hedge.

He chuckled with keen amusement.

'You told them to send this to London, and I got hold of it. You don't miss much, Bruce, I'll say that. However . . .' He started to run his plump fingers about the wide hem of the skirt, which was very full and pleated. He talked as if to himself. 'She didn't have a lot of time to change in, and she may have left something behind. Let me see, let me . . .'

He stopped abruptly, picked a penknife from the desk

and slit the hem for a few inches. Then he inserted a finger, and Mary and I heard the rustle of paper. He drew the paper out—it was a little folded sheet—and flattened it on the desk.

'Well?' I snapped, and went forward.

And then I had a shock, and I heard Mary—also by the desk—draw in a sharp breath. Pinky kept quite still as he looked down on that sheet of paper and the absurd little drawings on it. There were fully forty of them, none any larger than a postage stamp, and all the same.

They were drawings of an invalid chair.

6
Denyer is Co-opted

Had it not been for what we already knew I think all of us would have laughed, but there was nothing laughable in that series of pen-drawings.

Pinky pushed the sheet aside abruptly.

'Well, well,' he barked. 'So they make us a present of a sheet of drawings. I wonder why?'

'Could they be pass-signs?' Mary asked.

'They could,' I said, 'but it isn't likely. If Elsa could put the skirt up as a guide to send us the wrong way, she's not beyond leaving this deliberately sewn in the hem of her garment. Eh, sir?'

'That's the obvious thing for us to think,' Holt agreed. 'The obvious thing is to ignore these. However, these people have peculiar minds. They may get as far as guessing that we'll suspect it is a catch, but not as far as wondering whether we'll assume it isn't because it looks very much as if it is.' He opened a drawer in his desk, took out a small pair of scissors, and cut three of the little drawings from the sheet; he handed these to me, then cut and handed another three to Mary. 'Now you've got 'em. That can't do any harm. Er . . .' He dropped the rest of the drawings into the drawer, as if carelessly, and leaned back. 'I've given orders for that quay at Hansea to be guarded, and none of the refugees are to be taken to billets or centres until each and every one has been thoroughly examined and their clothes searched. Either of you any other ideas?'

My mind was a blank, except that a pretty profile seemed to haunt me.

'When we get a description of the woman from Denyer,' said Mary, 'the police can put out a call for her.'

'Hmm,' grunted the Pink 'Un. 'She'll be disguised so that we'd never recognise her. I think the chief hope for the moment is Ernst. And wherever the Withered Man goes, trouble follows.' He broke off and smiled. 'Oh, well. You two go to Bruce's flat. I'll send young what's-his-name round there when I've finished with him. He's perfectly all right,' added the Pink 'Un. 'I've been fully into his credentials, and he's as safe as houses.'

'Meaning,' I said, 'that you think we should use him.'

'He knows Elsa,' said Holt. 'He's one of the few who have really seen her at close quarters. Except the refugees, and we can't use them. All right, all right,' he roared. 'Don't stand there wasting my time, get off with you.'

I felt deflated when I went downstairs, and called a cab for the Park Lane flat. It was a silent run, and we were not particularly cheered when we saw the Lagonda standing outside the building.

Percy had been watching from the window, and opened the door before I took my keys out.

' 'Mornin', sir,' he said brightly. ' 'Mornin', Miss Dell. 'Ad a nice run in the be-ootiful country?' He chuckled, but his expression grew sober. 'I got to apologise about me be'aviour this mornin', Guv'nor. I don't know what come over me, strike me if I don't. Hupset, that's what it was, hupset I wasn't going to be a witness of the ceremony. 'Ow's the old boy? Did you get a caning?'

What can you do with a man like that? I had to force myself not to smile.

'Percy,' I said, 'you'll overstep the line one of these days and when you do you'll be thrown out on your neck. Go and get some coffee.'

'Lunch is all ready, sir,' said Percy triumphantly. 'I got a bit o' steak, an' I've done some chips.'

'Serve it,' I said.

'It's on the 'ot-plate,' said Percy smugly, and he retired into his kitchen with an expression which clearly said that if I did not consider he had made amends I was unreasonable.

I had not realised how hungry I was, and Mary ate with relish. The feeling of deflation and of failure gradually faded.

The flat is a small one, with a main bedroom, a little cubby-hole which Percy uses, a dining-room and a small lounge. The lounge overlooks Hyde Park, and for that reason I like it, even though the trenches and the sandbagged A.A. gun stations are grim reminders of what is always at the back of our minds.

Sitting on the couch, drinking coffee, with Mary next to me, I said:

'A dozen times today I've felt that my eyes wouldn't keep open for another minute, and I know I dozed in the car. We'd set so much on today, and the jolt that Pinky gave us hasn't properly gone. But common sense says that a nap will do us more good than two hours' discussion. And we can't really move until young Denyer comes.'

On the face of it that may not seem like devotion to duty, but when you have been harassed from pillar to post as I have, when you've never been sure whether you would get an hour's sleep in the next twenty-four—or for that matter

41

forty-eight—you don't lose an opportunity for a doze.

I was soon in that pleasant, half-comatose state which precedes sleep. I felt Mary get up from the couch but did not have the energy to protest. She brought a rug from the bedroom and spread it over me carefully. I caught the aroma of a Virginia 3 cigarette after hearing the scrape of a match, and then I dropped off.

I awakened to a: 'Well, well, well!' in a deep and hearty voice, and I opened my eyes reluctantly. The fumes of sleep were still fogging my mind when Ted Angell went on heartily: 'Nero fiddled while Rome burned, Drake finished his game of bowls while Philip approached, and the great Bruce Murdoch sleeps while the Fifth Column marches unimpeded. Wake up, lout!'

'I am awake,' I said with what dignity I could muster. 'I've been thinking.'

'And this kept you warm while you did it,' said Ted, plucking the rug from my legs. 'Mary told me that she left you in here precisely two and a quarter hours ago.'

'Which time you've managed to get some respectable clothes on,' I observed. I stood up, stretched and yawned. 'Is Denyer here?'

'There was a 'phone call to say he'll be here at six o'clock.'

'That gives me twenty minutes,' I said, glancing at my watch. 'I'll have a bath.'

'Percy's running it,' said Ted. 'Between them, Mary and Percy spoil you impossibly.'

On top of the sleep the cold bath was just what I needed. By the time I was dressed and back in the lounge I felt capable of tackling anything and anyone.

At six precisely the front door bell rang.

Percy opened it, to admit young Denyer and Mick Fuller. Mick had changed into an immaculate silver grey suit, but Denyer had on the baggy flannels and the rumpled sports coat that I had seen that morning, and there was still a bead of sweat on his upper lip. He had big, hazel eyes, agleam with excitement.

'Jolly glad to see you again,' he said, and somewhat to my surprise he took and wrung my hand. 'By Jingo, didn't you put a move on this morning!'

'Thanks,' I said drily. 'Have you seen anyone in London?'

'I saw a funny little bald-headed fellow,' said Denyer, unaware of the sacrilege of that description of the Pink 'Un. 'He asked one or two footling questions, then sent me over here.'

'What did he ask?' I wanted to know.

'Oh, how many men had paid attention to the woman, and that kind of thing.'

It appeared that I had overestimated the intelligence of young Denyer.

'What was the answer?' I asked.

'Well . . .' He hesitated, as he sat on the edge of the couch. Mary had slipped into the room, and we were all present except Percy. 'She was a stunning-looking girl, you know. Really a peach, and she was always talking about her husband. I—er—well, never mind what I thought,' amended Denyer hastily. 'Naturally there was always a crowd of men about her.'

'How long had she been at the reception quay?'

'Oh, about a week.'

'Do refugees often stay as long as that?'

'Some do,' said Denyer. 'She told me that some of her relatives might turn up, and asked permission to stay until they arrived. It wasn't easy to refuse her.'

'What kind of a description of her did you give the funny little bald-headed man?'

'I'd got a photograph,' Denyer said proudly. 'He seemed tickled to death by that, and is having some copies made. She was about five foot five or six,' added Denyer. 'Very fair-haired—definitely the Scandinavian type. Or German,'

43

he amended. 'Very blue eyes, very regular features, although you'd say that her lips were rather full. But I just
can't believe that she was a spy,' cried Denyer. 'Oh, I know
she is, but she was actually wounded on her flight from
Amiens!'

'Where?' I snapped.

'A machine-gun bullet struck a glancing blow on the
back of her hand,' said Denyer. 'It didn't make much of a
wound, but it was there all right.'

'Right or left hand?' put in Mary.

'Left, but . . .'

'Oh, it matters,' I said. 'She'll have difficulty in hiding
the fact that she has a scar. That's good to know. You say
she was always with a crowd of men. Did you notice anyone who paid her particular attention?'

'Two or three hung around her more than the others,
until they were taken off to their billets.'

'Do you know what areas these men went to?'

'Yes, of course. I was partly responsible for sending
them.'

'Your first job for us,' I said, 'is to visit those billeting
areas and to look over the refugees. Any men or women
who spent a lot of time with Elsa need questioning.'

Denyer's eyes glistened.

'I'll do it like a shot!'

'Active service at last,' I said drily. 'I don't know what
else we'll want from you, but there may be quite a lot of
odds and ends. Is there any news of Father André?'

Denyer's smile disappeared.

'He was dead when you left, according to the doctor.
It seemed such a senseless crime, although I suppose he
knew something about this Withered Man, and she knew he
might talk about it. That's common sense, isn't it?'

'Yes indeed! Did you ever talk to Father André about
the man?'

'Well, only in snatches. It was a kind of spare-time job

44

for me, you know. He'd seen this withered fellow in Dieppe waiting for a boat for England. The boat only arrived yesterday.'

'Did Elsa contact with anyone from it?'

'With a man she said was her father,' said Denyer. 'He was brought ashore on a stretcher, and went straight out to the hospital.'

'Hospital!' I shouted, and Denyer looked startled. 'A man on a stretcher, old enough to be her father! What's the name of the hospital?'

'The—the Hansea Cottage Hospital, of course. It's the only one for miles.'

Ted was already at the 'phone, getting a call through to the hospital, and it came quickly. I took the receiver, and asked several pertinent questions. There had been no patient from the camp on a stretcher. One or two had come in an ambulance, but no ambulance had reported the previous night.

'Thank you,' I said, ringing off. Denyer was staring at me wide-eyed. 'Do you know the number of the ambulance the man went on?' I almost prayed.

'I—I don't, I'm afraid,' replied Denyer. 'But it certainly left.'

'Oh, it left,' I said bitterly. 'Carrying with it the Withered Man. God knows where it is now.'

I had a call put through to Hansea, and arranged for the police to try to trace the ambulance. Denyer was able to tell me the time it had left the quay, and with luck there would be news of it. Even as I telephoned I was appalled by the thoroughness of the spy's arrangements.

'I hope I haven't made a bloomer,' said Denyer, uneasily.

'You've done all you could,' I assured him, and offered him a cigarette. He refused; his heart wouldn't stand smoking. I thought grimly that his heart was not going to stand much of the excitement likely to follow the trail of the

Withered Man. 'Now get busy on those billeting areas,' I said. 'Mick, will you go with him? If you need more help, the police or the L.D.V. will give it to you.'

Mick was not going to enjoy a house-to-house search among the billets of the refugees, but one of us had to be with Denyer. They lost no time, while soon after they had gone a message arrived from the Pink 'Un. In an envelope were half a dozen copies of the photograph which Denyer had secured. Denyer's word-description fitted Elsa Bruenning admirably. She was a Scandinavian beauty.

'Fair hair won't help us much, Bruce,' Mary warned. 'She'll be able to dye that in a matter of an hour.'

The telephone cut across her words, and Ted lifted it; he frowned, and handed the receiver to me.

'For Mr. Murdoch,' he said.

Something in Ted's expression puzzled, even troubled, me as I took the receiver and announced: 'This is Bruce Murdoch.'

I had never heard it before, yet it was just the voice I would have expected from this man who had grown so much in my mind. Slightly guttural, and yet sibilant especially with the letter 's'. Pitched on a key neither high nor low, very calm and confident. 'Mr. Murdoch, I am glad to have the opportunity of this vord with you. You have not, I trust, injured Ernst.'

I fought against tightness in my throat.

'Ernst is well cared for,' I said carefully.

'Which has the double meaning,' said the man at the other end of the wire, as Ted went into the next room, intent on tracing the call. 'You vill learn that I cannot allow you to haff double-meanings, Mr. Murdoch. You are a foolish young man. Already you haff gone rushing in the wrong directions very often. A dangerous habit, you vill agree.'

The Withered Man paused.

7

I am Threatened

I believe firmly that there is one thing which the English have brought to a fine art, and the Germans cannot comprehend. I have been told frequently that Germans have no sense of humour, but little that I know of them supports this contention. Their humour may be different from the British, but it exists. They have no sense at all of the facetious, however, and facetiousness is second nature to the English.

I say this as a Scotsman.

There was not much time for me to decide what attitude to adopt. I had no doubt of his identity, and wanted him on the telephone to give Ted a chance to trace the call. The best way to do that was to puzzle him. And so I became facetious.

'Well,' I said, 'the wrong direction often gets us to the right place. For instance, it got me to Ernst.'

'Vich vos the wrong place.'

'A matter of opinion,' I said lightly. 'I always think the chain-and-its-weakest-link story can be relied on. You know—a chain is as strong as . . .'

'Ach, you fool. Listen to me, Murdoch, I haff no time to vaste like you. Your activities in many places, they are known. You can be considered a dangerous man.'

'Nice of you,' I murmured.

'Vill you stop that voolings! Before the day iss out you will be a man dead!'

'Too bad,' I said.

I heard an oath that sounded like '*Ach Himmel*'.

'But there are things you and me could say to each other. I vould like to meet you,' the speaker said flatly.

47

'Awkward,' I retorted, 'as I'm going to be dead.'

'You vill die unless you do exactly vot I say.'

'My dear man,' I said, 'this is London, England. You are in constant danger, with a considerable number of armed men looking for you. You have a few idiots who work for you, but if Ernst is a fair example idiot is the right word. I shall live for a long time.'

I expected a bellowed reply, but received none. After a few seconds I asked:

'Are you still there?'

There was still no answer, and I knew that he had gone. I banged the telephone platform up and down and a girl's voice came quietly:

'He rang down immediately after you said "a long time". I have a verbatim copy of the conversation. Would you like me to read it back?'

'No, thank you,' I growled. 'But I would like a copy.'

Ted came in at that point, his expression showing that he was pleased with himself.

'It was from a call-box in Staines,' he announced. 'I've told the Yard, and they're getting busy. The devil of it is we can't give a reliable description of the beggar. On the whole, what do you make of it?' he demanded.

I looked at Mary.

'He's so close to us that Mick and Denyer might have been followed,' she remarked.

'Yes, sweet,' said I, 'but Pinky will have Denyer and Mike followed, there's no need to worry about anything happening to them.'

'What do we do now?' asked Ted.

Mary's eyes sparkled.

'Bruce *could* get some more sleep!'

'For that,' I retorted, 'you'll pay excessively.' I ran my hand through my hair, and went on with what I hope was commendable briskness: 'Obviously, we go to Staines. It's pretty sure to be what the Withered Man wanted me to do.'

48

Ted is a bright lad in some respects but things often take a long time to sink into him.

'Why the deuce do you say that?' he demanded.

'Because, my oaf,' I said, 'he would not have telephoned me at all had he not wanted me to know where he was. He must have known that the call would be traced. It is typically German. A trick succeeds once, and he assumes it always will. He led me after Ernst by the display of the skirt; now he leads me to Staines by the telephone call.'

'It's very involved,' grumbled Ted. 'And anyhow if you think that's true why go to Staines?'

'Because I believed one thing the gentleman says: he wants to see me.'

'Yes,' Mary said slowly. 'And he also wants to kill you.'

'Between wanting and doing,' said I, putting an arm about her shoulders, 'there is a very large gap. I have a feeling the W.M. will find it. The plan of campaign is simplicity itself. I'm going to Staines in the Lagonda, with Percy driving. I fancy I shall be followed. You two will come after me.'

'I'm coming with you!' said Mary at once.

'No,' I said, with a show of indifference I was a long way from feeling. 'There must be intelligence in the rear as well as in the van, and I can't trust Ted to do the right thing in emergency.' I winked at Ted, hoping that Mary would not see it, and rang for Percy. To my surprise he was in his chauffeur's uniform except for his cap, which he held in his left hand.

'All ready ter start, sir.'

Percy was determined that he must maintain his good behaviour to counteract his misdemeanours of the morning. Both he and Ted went out, and I took Mary's hands.

We should have been man and wife by then. Instead we were facing a risk as deadly as any we had unknown. There was no doubt in either of our minds as to the danger to come from the Withered Man. Both of us were far beyond the stage of thinking 'it can't happen here'. There *was* a Fifth Column, and this man was an executive of it. In London, perhaps the whole of England, he had more power and more striking force than any gang leader in Chicago during Prohibition.

Mary's eyes were suspiciously bright. I was superficially brisk and confident.

'Darling,' I said, 'you're getting worked up over nothing at all. I'm armed, and you and Ted will be behind me. This man may have an organisation but he's not all-powerful.'

'Bruce, for God's sake be careful,' she pleaded. 'The man frightens me.'

'He has developed a psychological angle to the spreading of rumour and false news,' said I. We both suspected that we would go through fire and blood before our hands gripped again. I can only put these facts down, and not try to explain them, but all I added was: 'Keep close to my heels.'

Mary nodded, and Ted banged unnecessarily on the door.

When downstairs, I tried to avoid looking up at the small window, but failed. Mary was there. I could see her smiling. I lit a cigarette, and climbed into the rear seat.

Percy let in the clutch.

By my side were our gas-masks—service type—steel helmets and the oddments that constant danger makes it necessary to carry about. At one time they gave confidence: now I have used them so often that they seem a natural part of life's equipment.

'There's a Lancia just takin' orf behind us,' said Percy.

I nodded, and manœuvred so that I could see the car in the driving mirror. It was a modern one, and the driver was a youthful-looking man with long, yellow hair.

'Drive twice through Hyde Park,' I ordered.

Percy obeyed, and after the first lap the Lancia pulled

away and no longer followed us. But soon afterwards, when we were going along the Bayswater Road, I saw it just behind me. At the other side of Hammersmith Broadway, however, it had gone. I frowned, for I was convinced the Lancia had been following us. And then I stopped frowning, and contemplated—in the mirror—the large Austin now on our heels.

It followed as far as the end of the Great West Road.

There, at the fork road where you can take your choice between Slough and Staines, I saw the Austin pull into the side of the road, but the trick was not done successfully. A few yards ahead of the spot where the Austin stopped a Wolseley was parked. I saw its driver glance at the man in the Austin, and then the Wolseley started in our wake.

'Percy,' I said, 'the Wolseley is after us now, and we're approaching a spot where we can turn off the main road and get out of the traffic. Take the first turning right.'

Percy nodded.

'And that reminds me,' I said apropos of nothing, 'how did you know that we were coming out?'

'I 'appened to 'ear Teddy—I mean Mr. Angell—asking for the call to be traced,' said Percy. 'I put two an' two together, sir. Like me outfit?'

'How many guns does it carry?' I demanded darkly.

'Two,' said Percy brightly, 'and there's a box of hand grenades under the seat *you're* sittin' in, just in case of accident.'

Percy's tone suggested: 'Put that in your pipe and smoke it'. In spite of the close attention of the Wolseley I smiled at the thought of a box of hand grenades—which we carried as we so often worked in France and near the front line. In this unprecedented war there are no rules followed, and a secret agent might find himself chasing an enemy spy on to the battlefield just as easily as an Allied force might meet a convoy of Nazis on the road behind its own lines, and *vice versa*. It is like a gigantic war in which

guerilla tactics are being used all the time on an unprecedented scale.

'There's a turn,' Percy said.

He drove to the turning before swinging across the road
without giving any signal, and at the speed we were travelling that brought the Wolseley close to our rear wings. The
driver had to swing violently into the side, and had the
nerve to swear wildly at us. But two hundred yards along
the narrow road Percy had chosen he was on our heels
again.

'Percy,' I said, 'I want to be taken prisoner but I don't
want them to know I want it. Put up a show of resistance
but no more.'

Percy nodded.

It was half-past seven, and still broad daylight. We were
driving between fields in which a few labourers were still
working, but there was no traffic, and the hum from the
main road was barely audible. As soon as we were out of
sight of the main road and the workers, I said:

'Slow down, Percy. Have you seen anything of Mr.
Angell lately?'

'Not since Chiswick,' said Percy.

I had little time to think of Ted or Mary, for the Wolseley
swung round a corner and had to pull in sharply to avoid
a collision. The driver gave himself hardly time to jam
on his brakes before opening the door and rushing towards
us. His head and his hands were bare, and he was dressed
in a light grey lounge suit. He was no more than twenty-
three or four. At the same moment the rear doors of the
Wolseley opened, and two men spilled out.

The driver said cockily:

'Too bad, Murdoch, you were awake but not fast enough.
Get back into the car and drive straight on. You'll sit in
the front with your chauffeur. Meltze, get in the back and
keep them covered.'

'Why, you bloody Nazi . . .' Percy began and went on colourfully for a moment or two.

All that happened in a narrow lane on the outskirts of London, with civilian and military traffic not half a mile away, and Ted and Mary somewhere along the road.

At least, I hoped they were.

8

I Meet the Enemy

I felt more excited than scared.

That may have been because I knew that had they intended to kill they would have chosen that moment. For some reason the Withered Man did not want me dead for a while.

Percy was growling under his breath, and I said sharply and in a tone he would not mistake:

'Don't try any tricks, Percy!'

The man Meltze grunted, but I couldn't give in too easily. I made a grab for my steel helmet, on the seat now behind me. Meltze jammed a gun against the side of my face enough to scrape the skin. I rammed the hat on my head, then became aware of the *boom!* of an explosion behind us, unpleasantly like the crump of a high-explosive bomb. Dirt, dust and débris flew about, and there was a sheet of flame not a hundred yards behind.

The thudding of the débris quietened, and I searched the skies. I saw nothing, and there was no sign of aircraft, no bursting of anti-aircraft shells or the barking of the guns as they fired.

'It was us. We blow up the road,' Meltze stated flatly.

Looking over my shoulder I saw the Wolseley on our

heels, and the dust settling behind it. Later I was told, but even then I realised what Meltze meant. To prevent our being followed they had blown a crater in the road. I needed no more telling how thorough the Withered Man was, nor that he could rely entirely on his men. But perhaps the most astounding thing was his confidence: how dared he do this in England?

I glanced at Percy.

He nodded, imperceptibly, and his left hand sought for the dial of the small radio-transmitter with which the Lagonda was fitted. He made it look as if he were winding the clock, and to aid the deception I said:

'It's no use winding that thing. It stops every hour.'

'Well, I c'n *try*,' said Percy.

Trying, he started to tap against the dashboard, short and long taps which would give the London receiving station our position, and told them of the danger. Meltze appeared to notice nothing, and after some minutes Percy stopped. We had done all we could without asking for more trouble.

Meltze leaned forward.

'Turn here,' he ordered.

A narrow turning apparently led across barren fields but amid a copse of trees some distance off I saw the red roof of a house, smoke curling from a chimney. The road was bad, and I knew that even then Percy was cursing the effect on the car. With the September sun low in the west, a few fleecy white clouds drifting across the sky, and the distant hum of traffic on the English roads, anything else seemed impossible. It is hard to believe in one's own death.

The Wolseley kept within ten yards of us.

There was a big house among the trees, approached by a better road from the other direction. I caught glimpses of the river, and judged that the house was no more than half a mile from it. Now that we were almost on top of the place

I could see other buildings within sight and earshot. We were in one of those little oases of residential property built apparently with only one object: to make it as difficult as possible for the occupants to get to shops or stations. The Home Counties are littered with such 'estates'.

The rough road led through a gateway, and the Wolseley stopped for the young man to jump down and close the gate. By the time he was back in the car we had reached the front door. Meltze did not let us move until the others had arrived. Then he said:

'All right, you can get down.'

As we climbed to the carriage-way of a surprisingly large house, Meltze tapped our coats for guns, and took mine as well as Percy's two. Percy was finding it a hard job to keep the peace. His lips were set and his chin thrust forward, and his physiological villainy was at its most expressive stage.

'How careful you were,' said the driver of the Wolseley. 'I am surprised at you, Murdoch. If I had given you a chance you would have used these.'

'I'll get the chance,' I said.

'Don't run away with *that* idea,' he retorted. His English was not only good, it was native. Had I seen him walking down an English street I would have said that he was a typical youngster of the higher social order, and I will swear that he was Public School. I was so used to treachery in all forms that it did not shock me.

'And don't sneer,' he snapped. 'You're clinging to an old regime, Murdoch, which is dying fast. It's been dead from the neck up for years, and now it's losing everything else it ever had.'

That was the moment when I registered a personal hatred for that young man. Already he was an enemy, and a ruthless one. But enemies—even pro-Nazis—are usually impersonal. I sometimes think that this war would have

55

been over quickly, and even could have been prevented, had the English been more capable of hatred.

He bent an arm and cracked his elbow into my ribs. The blow not only hurt, but sent me reeling. It was an example of a sheer sadistic desire to hurt, and there was not even the excuse that he wanted to frighten me, or that he was after information.

'*That*,' said a woman from the door which had opened without my noticing it, '*is quite enough, Cator.*'

It was an attractive voice, slightly husky, and very clear. The English was good but obviously foreign, and in the utterance of the man's name there was a guttural which enabled me to place her nationality within reasonable limits. The black and white of Denyer's photograph did not do her justice, although his verbal picture of her had. Her complexion, pale and delicate, was superb. Her blue eyes had the starry-eyed loveliness which you find in a few English girls and far more often in Scandinavia, or in the Saxon type.

She was not particularly slim, and a light summer frock fell lightly over full breasts emphasised by her small waist. Her legs were very neat; bare toes showed through the loopholes of her sandals. Her hair was braided.

And *she* had murdered the *curé*.

She probably read the thoughts in my mind, for her lips curled, and then for the first time I saw that she was not beautiful all the time. The smile—if it could be called a smile—told more of the truth than her eyes did. It was quite inhuman. The man Cator obeyed her promptly, and stepped away from me.

'Take the chauffeur to the garage,' she said, and Percy was hustled from the front of the house, Cator grunted, 'Follow the woman,' and I obeyed.

In a high, well-lighted hall she stopped and looked at me for some seconds. I think I acted as naturally as if paying a social call. One gets used to emergencies, and I have often been in a position where the odds against escaping alive were very heavy. It does not create a lack of fear as much as a refusal to admit that things are as bad as they are.

'Yes,' she said critically, 'I think you will do.'

With that she laughed, a light and musical sound which somehow betrayed the smile on her lips. She went up a wide flight of stairs, and with Cator behind me I followed. I was keeping my eyes open, and from the landing window I saw a small car pass a road running alongside the house.

'In here,' said Elsa Bruenning.

She stepped aside for me to enter a room which was furnished heavily, as a study. Books lined two walls, and part of a third. There was a musty smell, as if it had been closed up for some time, but through the west wall window the sun was streaming, and reflecting on the glass of one of the bookshelves. The reflection was so clear and bright that it dazzled me.

The window was closed, and the room was quiet. A thick carpet muffled the sound of footfalls, and aided the impression of wealth and luxury. I turned towards the woman and Cator, who stood by the door. He kept his right hand in his pocket and I could see the snout of an automatic poking against his coat.

'Sit down,' said Elsa.

'Do you mind if I smoke?' I asked, and was surprised when she nodded.

'I will join you, Mr. Murdoch. Cator will make sure that you do nothing foolish.'

I brought out my case, which had a lighter built into it.

'I wouldn't rely too much on Cator if I were you,' I said. 'An Englishman who can work in England against England is fundamentally insecure and probably quite mad.' I flicked the lighter and lit her cigarette before lighting my own.

I saw Cator's cheeks flush; despite earlier appearances he was not yet a hardened renegade.

The woman said softly: 'Your tongue will get you into more trouble than need be.'

'Happily,' I said, 'this remains a free country, and speech is as free as the air. I . . .'

'You *fool*!' she shouted, taking a step towards me with a clenched hand uplifted. I regarded the small fist sardonically, but was also watching her flushed cheeks, the glitter in her eyes. She lowered her voice but went on with a fierce intensity which would have fascinated me in even more difficult circumstances. 'You *fool*!' she repeated. 'To talk of free speech and free people. There is none! None who are. They are all answerable to the Third Reich! This democracy, this leadership of a country by the masses, the herds of cattle . . .' The sneer which had made her look so vicious when I had first seen it was in evidence again. 'It had to end, and it is ending now. There is one creed, one master, one power!'

'Nazi-ism—the Führer—aggression,' I said mildly. 'We ought to make a song about it, didn't we? But spare me this absurdity, Fräulein Bruenning. The British don't lose wars.'

I thought she would strike me then. I believe she would have done. Past her I could see Cator, with a wolfish grin on his face, and his attitude was one great swagger. But before her uplifted fist fell, I heard something which affected me much more strongly and strangely than her threats. It seemed some distance off, but it was clear enough.

A *thump*—a pause—a *thump* again.

It must have been the silence in the room after my rejoinder to her outburst which exaggerated the sound, but it drowned all other things. I found myself waiting after the third thump for another. It came. Slowly, slowly, the thumping drew nearer. I felt a cold shiver run down my spine. My eyes were turned towards the door, for I knew there was a man approaching, I knew how he was coming, and who he was.

Thump—thump—thump—
Thump!

This time it was just outside the door. I stared towards it, seeing the handle turning slowly and waiting tensely for the next thud. None came for several seconds. The handle seemed an unbearable time making a full turn. Then, as slowly, the door opened. I saw the iron ferrule of an ebony walking-stick poke through.

Deliberately, I turned about.

For one thing, my breath was coming in sharp gasps which made me seem afraid, although fear was not in me then. For another, I felt my cheeks go pale. For a third, what little self-control I retained told me that it was essential—vital!—that the man entering the room should not see that he had made such an impression.

I stepped to the window, and slipped my hand in my pocket. I realised that my cigarette was dead in my mouth, and drew out the lighter and flicked it into flame. At the same time the door banged back against the wall and the *thump,* deadened by the thick carpet, echoed in my ears.

Drawing in smoke helped to calm me.

Without seeing the garden I looked down into it. I saw Cator reach the wall close to the window; he had his gun in his hand and showing, as if prepared to stop my movement. I ignored him as I ignored the others. In my ears was the sound of heavy, laborious breathing. I would not have been surprised to learn that it was from an animal.

Then the guttural, even-pitched voice which I had heard over the telephone came from behind me.

'You find int'rest in der garden, Murdoch?'

My breathing grew easier. The absurd, momentary panic

59

had gone although I had been compelled to remind myself sharply, urgently, that this was a man. The blood was back in my cheeks, and I did not find it hard to appear nonchalant. I turned to face him.

'Yes,' I said. 'More than I find in here.'

That was how I first encountered the Withered Man.

My mental images had inspired all manner of wild conjectures, and the sight of him had an unexpected effect—that of relief. For one thing, I knew him. Yet I could see why men were afraid of him, and I could even understand something of the power he had of enveloping others in a telepathic aura of fear.

I think the weapon which Baron Ludvic von Horssell uses to greatest effect is a psychological one, and I have never seen him, never been aware of his presence near me, without feeling a faint echo of the panic which seized me when I first heard the sound of his approach.

He was tall, but his breadth and depth of shoulder and chest, and the fact that he leaned forward heavily on his stick, robbed him of some inches. I thought at first that he was bald, but I saw soon that his hair was grey, in fact almost white, and cropped very close to his head, so that one could see the layers of flesh which piled upon each other. His forehead slanted backwards, but the effect of that was emphasised by his prominent, jet black eyebrows, a bushy tangle of thick hair.

His eyes were set deeply beneath those prominent brows, and were unexpectedly large and clear. They were also cold and, although I know they are blue, as the light from the window shone on him they seemed colourless.

His nose was straight but short and large at the tip, and the nostrils were plainly visible as I looked straight at him. I could see the matt of hairs just inside them. His upper lip was short because of the thick, flat effect of his mouth, and his chin was prominent—as near an image of Mussolini's as I have ever seen. The massive head was set on the big shoulders with hardly a neck. When he turned, I saw the flattened back of his head.

If ever a man typified the Prussian, he did.

He was dressed in clerical grey, and wore a winged collar with a cravat fastened by a solitaire diamond ring. His face seemed equal, on either side, but from the shoulder downwards it was easy to see the ravages of paralysis. His right arm was loose at his side, the hand curled and the flesh white and bloodless. Although he stood upright he lurched on his right side, and I saw that the shoe—or boot —on his right foot was small and made of different leather from that of his left boot.

That was the man I saw, leaning heavily on the ebony stick and staring at me expressionlessly, unless there was a hint of cold curiosity.

I do not know whether he was surprised by my manner, or my faint smile. He moved his gaze first, then began to move towards a large chair by the window, each movement slow, his left leg treading the carpet with surprising gentleness, and the *thump* coming as he banged his stick. It was a crawling motion for his right leg dragged behind him, and it was clear that he was in pain as he moved it up. Without speaking he reached the chair, which had a long footrest. He lowered himself into it, dropping the last few inches, then used one hand to lift that pitiful withered leg on to the rest. Only then did he acknowledge my presence again.

'So you see,' he said, 'we meet. You are to learn, Murdoch, vot so many others have learned. *Alvays* I am right. Do you remember I told you vot vould happen to you before the day vos over?'

9

Baron Ludvic von Horssel

I knew instinctively that he must not gain a mental or psychological ascendancy. He was a man who ruled and controlled by the power of fear, and I had to make sure that the yoke did not slip on to my shoulders. I smiled.

'I think it depends,' I said, 'on who wanted the meeting first. Presumably you developed an urge to see me after I had started on the fräulein's trail, whereas I've been wanting to see you for a long time.'

The big eyebrows knitted.

'You did not know of me.' He spoke as if there was not the slightest chance of his being wrong.

'You underestimate my department, Baron.' I was quite safe in the use of that title, although this man had given it up soon after the rise of the National Socialists to power. I had seen his photographs a dozen times, and he was in the archives at Whitehall as a man who had worked long after 1918 for the lost cause of the Hohenzollern dynasty. I knew that in those days he had been hale and hearty, and I wondered where he had lost the use of his right leg and arm.

The 'Baron' startled him, and I heard Cator draw in a sharp breath.

'So,' said Baron Ludvic von Horssell, 'you know of me.'

'Who does not?' I asked politely.

I could see the faint bewilderment in those almost colourless eyes, and inwardly rejoiced. I stepped to the desk in the corner opposite him and leaned against it after stubbing the glowing end out. I could see not only the Withered Man but Elsa Bruenning and Cator. All were staring at me with flattering intensity.

'Many do not,' said von Horssell heavily.

'Only the illiterate masses,' I said sardonically. 'The beasts who should be trodden underfoot, Baron! However, you wanted to see me, presumably to talk. I will advise you to hurry.'

He pushed his head forward.

'Vy should I hurry?'

'Because my friends should not be long,' I said. 'Although I have some influence I imagine the Government will prefer to have you under lock and key.'

He lifted his left hand and gripped the lapel of his coat.

'Let it be clear that no one vill find you here, Murdoch,' he said. 'It is quite safe, and one of many places where I can be as I vould in my own Fatherland. You are not aware of der many sympathisers with the Fatherland in dis country. Besides der road vos blown up behind you.'

'There are two ways to most given places,' I said. 'The explosion was a mistake. It will attract attention, and I should imagine that there is a strong cordon about the vicinity already. You'd be surprised,' I added, 'how many people do not sympathise with the Fatherland. Moreover,' I went on earnestly, 'my car carries a radio-transmitter. I was able to send out directions quite easily.'

The hand waved.

'Talk,' said von Horssell. 'Do me the privilege of believing I take care of all things that can go wrong, Murdoch. I vill explain. Two cars, like your own and vit' the same number of passengers, haff been sent in different directions. Your radio vos expected, and cut out. No, Murdoch, none know that you are here.'

It was not only the words that sent a shiver down my spine. It was the quiet assumption of certainty, the fact that von Horssell took it for granted that precautions would be made but overcome; he did not allow the possibility that anything could go wrong.

Elsa interrupted for the first time since von Horssell's arrival.

'That is different from what you expected.'

'Fräulein,' I said earnestly, 'I have learned to expect everything. The Baron likes to believe that nothing can go wrong.' I shrugged. 'It is a comforting belief for him, and I would hate to make an incapacitated man uncomfortable.'

I fancied I saw a change in her expression. I thought then, and afterwards proved, that it was admiration mingled with surprise. It is pleasant to be admired by a beautiful woman. She was surprised—as were the others —by the fact that anyone could face what appeared to be certain disaster with equanimity, which is one of the best English characteristics. I have lived most of my life in England, and my mother was English: I can share that characteristic in some measure.

Von Horssell gripped his lapel again. It would take a lot to shake him out of his colossal self-confidence.

'I have controlled everything,' he declared. 'You vill not be found. But—today I told you that I vould like to see you. It vos for good reasons. But . . .' His eyes narrowed, and for the first time he showed expression: it was not so much hate as malevolence, a personal malevolence. 'It is my misfortune to be disabled on one side. I do not like references to that disablement. You understand?'

I did, only too well.

I shrugged.

'I don't like being threatened,' I said, simply.

Von Horssell eased himself a little to one side. Doing so his lips tightened, and I was even more sure he was in constant pain. That was one of the most surprising things about the man. He ignored his own disadvantages, triumphed over a disability which to most men would have been complete. It was part of his immense strength: an utter refusal to accept defeat.

'Murdoch,' he said, 'you haff one chance, and one only, of living from now on. I can haff you sent from der room, and you vill never see daylight again. You vill die, and no one, not even your friends, vill know vot hass happened to you.'

The prickle of fear ran down my spine again.

'So,' he said, 'knowing that I vould say things to you that I vould not to many. I vould tell you that in some weeks—it may be months, but it vill be dis year—the beloved Führer will be in London, and the Fatherland will be in control of all der Empire of England. It is not like it vos in der last war. Now we haff der people and der weapons, der strength and der opportunity. You are losing der war, and you vill continue to lose it. Perhaps there vill for a while be an established Government in Canada, or Australia, but it vill not last. Der British Empire is breaking, and breaking fast.'

For the life of me I could not laugh at him, or scoff. He made it sound damnably convincing, the more so because there was none of the bluster and the bragging characteristic of so many Nazi leaders.

'And so, Murdoch, I can talk this way to you,' he went on. 'You are not der fool. Many times you haff worked against me and all that I stand for. You haff had victories. But none of them lasted. Always there were defeats to follow. Now—you, and your man Holt, become der nuisance. But for Holt, I believe that the march of der Fatherland vould be faster. Also—he is in the confidence of your Government.'

'Well?' I said.

'And so I say this to you. Vork, yes—but vork for *me*. Vork—but not for der dying body of a decayed Empire, a peoples which are soft in body and in mind, a richness which has become bloated vit' its own wealth.' Now his voice rose, he began to shout. 'Vork for der new day, Murdoch! Der chance is yours, and it vill not come again.'

65

He stopped, breathing hard after the shouting. But had they been whispered words they could not have startled me more, and I stared incredulously at a man who knew so little about the English that he could imagine this thing possible.

Then I looked at Cator, and understood why.

.   .   .   .

My first reaction was to say what I thought of Cator, and what von Horssell could do with his invitation. One of Pinky's rules came to my rescue, as it often did. 'Never let the other man know what you're thinking,' Pinky would say, 'even if it's obvious that you ought to be thinking it.'

Von Horssell's eyes were narrowed, and Elsa was staring at me. I thought desperately, and already the germ of an idea was in my mind.

I said: 'You hardly expect me to take that seriously, Baron.'

'Iss there any other vay in which you can live?'

'Life isn't everything,' I said.

'No?' said von Horssell. 'It iss the only thing that most of us haff got. It is the only thing *you* haff got.' He shifted his position again. 'You vill not haff it for long unless you make up your mind to accept vot I am suggesting. In an England which is properly controlled and governed by der methods of the Führer you could haff a position of power and authority over life and possessions. You need haff no fears of what vill happen. You vould be under my protection, Murdoch.'

I said: 'A lot of Nazis could turn in their graves at that. Can you remember Ernst and Rhoem?'

He waved his hand. Throughout the whole interview he showed little facial expression, and his lips only moved to speak, never to smile.

'That vos the past. They vere traitors to the Nazi regime,

to the great Führer. There vos a time ven I did not vork for him. But that iss not brought against me now, an' vill not be brought against you. Loyalty to the Third Reich from the time you start working for it, that is all.'

'It's asking too much,' I said decisively.

But I had shown sufficient hesitation to make von Horssell think that I was in two minds. I spent some minutes in rejecting the offer, telling him that I would rather be killed, even with a bullet in my back. During that harangue I saw Elsa's lips move in her peculiar, sensuous smile. Von Horssell heard me out, then picked up his ebony stick.

He poked it towards me, and the brass ferrule just touched my stomach.

'You vill go to anudder room and think of it,' he said. 'I offer you life, wealth, position, honour—or I offer you death. Cator—you vill take him away.'

I stepped towards the door with alacrity, but once there I hesitated as if I was about to speak. Then I changed my mind, and let Cator hustle me out.

In the passage was one of the men who had come from the Wolseley, armed and on guard. I went upstairs with Cator's gun prodding in my back. He pushed me by the shoulder into a small bedroom. As I straightened up I turned on him, and let myself go.

'You unprincipled swine! What the devil do you mean by that? If ever I work for him I'll handle you!'

I stopped abruptly, as if I wished that I had not spoken, and Cator sneered:

'You seem to have changed your ideas pretty quickly. And I do *believe* in Nazi-ism; you'd turn just to save your rotten skin.'

He slammed the door and I heard the key turn in the lock and Cator's footsteps stamping away. He had the German habit of thudding on his heels.

I turned to the one small window, about on a level with my head.

Standing on the foot of the single bed, I could see the garden, a pleasant patch of antirrhinums and late roses, with smooth lawns leading to the road some sixty yards from the front door. I saw two cars pass the gate, although there was no chance of being seen from the cars—a high hedge hid the window from the road except at the narrow gap by the gate—and I realised that I could not hear the engines. That was odd enough to make me examine the glass, and I knew from its peculiar yellowish tinge that it was soundproof and probably bullet-proof. There was no question of accepting von Horssell's offer—that may sound obvious, but also may be a necessary statement. I do not doubt the sincerity of my thoughts—that I would rather be killed that day than turn a hand against England.

But could I make von Horssell believe I had accepted?

Could I earn a reprieve for myself and at the same time find an opportunity for working *inside* von Horssell's organisation?

I found my thoughts came easily and logically. The obvious conclusion was that von Horssell would be a difficult if not impossible man to deceive. I might convince him that I was anxious to save my own life, but that would not help to prove that I was prepared to make a complete *volte face*. He would give me some kind of a test, some task which would implicate me in such a way that my erstwhile friends would become enemies.

I began to feel that it would be impossible to play von Horssell at his own game of duplicity and treachery without committing myself too far.

I finished one cigarette and lighted another. I wished there was some water for drinking, but the carafe on the bedside table was empty. I scowled as I stood up and stepped again to the window, and I had been looking out only for a few seconds when I heard footsteps outside the door.

My heart beat fast.

68

Was von Horssell sending for his final answer? Was that the only opportunity I should get for reaching a decision —or more accurately for working out a plan of campaign?

The door opened abruptly.

I stayed by the window, expecting to see Cator or Elsa. I was fully prepared for Elsa to try feminine wiles to persuade me. There is no originality in the Prussian, beyond a certain point. The idea that a woman could work on a man, that a beautiful woman was bound to have some success, was invariable. And so I imagined von Horssell would think, and I had a shock when I heard a familiar Cockney voice, and saw Percy pushed into the room.

He lost his balance when he struck against a chair, and went sprawling. The fall, the chair hitting against the wall, and Percy's round oaths drowned the sound of the locking of the door. I went to help him up, but he managed without my assistance, and stood for a moment glaring at the door. I really think he would have thrown himself at the thick panels had I not said:

'That won't help you.'

I spoke sharply for two reasons. It was the only way to make Percy look away from the door, and it was necessary because I was by then convinced that whatever was said in the room could be overheard. There was one clear reason why Percy should be put in with me—to force us into conversation so as to overhear what we said.

I seemed to see von Horssell's expressionless eyes, to see the animal curl on Elsa's lips.

Percy drew a deep breath.

'The perishing barstids,' he said. 'If I could git my 'ands round that swine's froat I'd squeeze 'im to pulp. Calls hisself an Englishman. English!' snorted Percy, and he glared at me.'Wot the 'ell are we going to do now?'

'We can't do much yet,' I said.

'We'll find a way out of this ruddy place in no time, and then I'll . . .'

'Don't talk nonsense,' I said sharply. 'We can't get out. These people sent other cars to distract any pursuit, and we're completely isolated.'

Percy's glare disappeared, and an expression that positively hurt me showed in his blue eyes. He was completely at a loss. His lips opened, and then he closed them again and licked them. His hand went to his pocket and he brought out the green packet of the cigarettes which he insists on smoking although he could well afford a better brand.

'Why, Guv'nor, I . . .'

'Don't talk for the sake of it,' I snarled. 'And don't blether about getting out of here—we can't. I wish to God I could get out of the blasted country, and find some peace.'

And as I spoke Percy gaped again, and his eyes showed *horror*—horror at the thought of hearing words like that from me. I turned abruptly, for I could not look at him without giving myself away and I was prepared to believe that we were watched as well as overheard.

While Percy said clearly: 'Gor *blimey*! 'Ave they torn *your* guts aht too?'

10

A Time for Seduction

The phrase was the complete expression of the thoughts in Percy's mind and he could not have put them more strongly nor more tersely. The horror had gone from his eyes, I saw when I glanced round, and he showed only disgust. There was one thing against which his loyalty would break—my own disloyalty, even by word.

'Hold your tongue!' I snapped.

Percy swallowed a lump in his throat, and felt for his

matches. He struck one, lit his cigarette, and drew in a mouthful of smoke. I was not looking at him, but I could sense that his eyes were on me, and that second thoughts were nagging him. He was looking for a catch, and just then I did not want him to find one.

'Guv'nor,' he said pleadingly, 'it ain't as bad as that. Even if they 'ave stopped the others from coming, we sent aht that call.'

I straightened up and looked at him squarely.

'It was cut out,' I said. 'Get this into your head. We haven't a chance of getting out of here. I knew this swine was thorough, but I didn't dream he was anything like this.'

Percy's blue eyes narrowed so that they almost disappeared, and deliberately he turned his back on me and sat at the end of the bed. The minutes passed while he smoked two cigarettes, and started to take out a third.

'Stop fidgeting,' I barked.

His hand stopped moving. Out of the corner of my eye I saw him looking at me blankly at first, and then covertly. I could have sent some message to him—I could have winked enough to make his sharp wits see what I was driving at, but Percy must not know what was in my mind. He can be read as easily as an open book, and if he feels light-hearted nothing in the world will stop him showing it.

Relief came at last in the form of Cator, who took Percy out. Percy looked at me once, in appeal, but my expression was blank.

I eased my collar when he had gone, for the room was stuffy and thick with smoke. Despite that I lit a cigarette, and then flung myself full length on the bed.

I turned drowsy.

I had been drowsy during the last few minutes when Percy had been in the room, and I had put it down to the airlessness of the little apartment, and to the strain that existed between us. But as I smoked, I remembered the sleep I had had that afternoon, and I knew that I should not be feeling so tired. I did not force myself to sit up and walk about the room, but just lay there, looking at the ceiling, and fighting against the fumes of exhaustion. 'Fighting' is only half true. I tried desperately not to close my eyes but I lacked the will to get up, or to move.

The cigarette dropped from my fingers, and I caught a faint smell of burning. That did stir me, and I found the cigarette and squeezed it between my fingers. The hot ash stung. I realised by then that I was being drugged, but my mind was too sluggish to worry about it. At last I closed my eyes, and they felt heavy, my head was aching dully. But sleep itself did not come, and I was aware of the opening of the door.

I heard Elsa's voice:

'He's right out. Get him to the other room.'

Someone grunted, and I felt hands gripping my legs and shoulders. But I could not open my eyes to see who it was, and by the time I was in the passage I was truly unconscious.

.　　　.　　　.　　　.　　　.

I do not know how long I slept, if it can be called sleep.

It was dark when I opened my eyes, and memory flooded back when I felt a sharp prickling at them, and the heavy weight which had seemed to be on them when I had lain on the bed. The darkness was comforting. When I moved my arm I felt the coolness of a sheet against my hand.

I groped, finding that I was in bed, with sheets, blankets and a feather eiderdown for cover. I kept quite still once I had confirmed that discovery, almost prepared to find that the visit to Staines and the talk with von Horssell had been a vivid nightmare.

And then I was aware of a light, even breathing nearby.

I jerked my head up, and tried to pierce the gloom, looking towards the sound of the breathing. I could see nothing at all, not even the faint outlines of my own bed. By then I felt the comfortable spring mattress, and the down pillow on which my head rested. Nothing had been spared for my comfort, but the knowledge of a companion was disconcerting.

I must have been lying there wide awake for nearly five minutes before I thought of feeling for a bedside lamp. There was one. I moved as silently as I could, but the *click!* as I pressed the switch was loud. I blinked against the subdued light, and then looked round towards the direction of the breathing.

Elsa was in the bed next to mine. She had been sleeping —I assumed that at all events—while turned towards me. Now her eyes were open and she stared at me, somewhat bemusedly I thought. One arm, bare to the shoulder, was stretched out over the bedspread. The skin was flawless and gleamed like satin beneath the light. Her hair was braided and in a net, and her lips were not touched with carmine.

'What . . .' I started.

Elsa smiled, and with a hand drawn from beneath the sheets stifled a yawn. It was all so natural that again I was forced to the weak belief that it was a dream. She said, in her husky, rather throaty voice:

'Is it late, darling?'

'Oh, my God!' I gasped. 'Am I crazy?'

'Crazy? Why?' asked Elsa. She eased herself up on her pillows and there was an amused expression in her eyes as she studied me. I knew that this was happening and that I was in full possession of my senses. But I could conceive of no reason, however crazy, for this bizarre situation. She stretched her arms above her head and I saw that she was wearing a primrose-coloured nightdress or pyjama jacket. Her expression was positively roguish, and it was hard to imagine the vicious smile I had seen several times.

'I give it up,' I said.

She laughed lightly, flung back the bedclothes, and stood for a moment between the beds. She wore pyjamas, and they did nothing at all to hide her figure, while the jacket was low-cut and flimsy. Quite suddenly she bent down and kissed me on the lips.

At the same moment there was a flash so brilliant that my eyes pained me, and the light from the bedside lamp seemed dim. Another flash, but as it finished I pushed a hand against her shoulder and pushed her roughly away. She sat abruptly on the side of her bed, but she was laughing at me.

I knew that flashlight photographs had been taken.

'What is this?' I said angrily. 'A lesson in seduction?'

'No,' said Elsa. 'A lesson in thoroughness. You will have to live a long while to outwit the Baron, you know.'

I was alert enough to growl: 'Who said anything about trying to outwit him?'

'A most sensible remark,' said Elsa mockingly. She leaned forward until her face was no more than a foot from mine, and her voice as well as her manner altered. 'It can be very pleasant working for us, Bruce.'

'Oh,' I said. 'Could it?'

'*Very* pleasant.' Elsa leaned back and stretched, her breasts taut against the silk of her pyjamas. 'The Baron has some faults but no one could ever call him jealous. How do you feel now?'

I stifled a temptation to say I felt fiercely angry.

'I could do with a cup of tea,' I found myself saying, and in a moment she twisted round and pressed a bell set in the wall behind her. I was trying to accustom myself to the madness of this situation and yet realised that in a measure even I was accepting it. Damn it, what could I do short of throwing a fit of melodramatic prudery?

'The English must have their tea.' This time her laugh

74

had a cruel note. 'They may not find it so easy in a few months' time. They *think* they're highly taxed now, but they will pay for the war. But we needn't go into that now,' she added, and she sat on the edge of my bed, looking down into my eyes for all the world as if I was the only man who mattered.

The door opened abruptly, and I heard a sharp command:

'*In there!*'

I stared towards the door, and then I went rigid, while Percy Briggs entered, bearing a tea-tray in his hands. He caught sight of me, and stopped short. I thought the tray would fall, but long practice made him retrieve it. He did not move for some seconds but I could sense what was passing though his mind. I have never wanted to shout so much in my life, have never been so desperately anxious to correct an impression, but I *knew* that I could not. I did not move nor speak as he deposited the tray on the bedside table. Between his set lips he hissed:

'*You ruddy swine!*'

Then he turned away.

I stared after him, feeling hot and cold in turn. It was Elsa who brought me back to myself.

'Forget him,' she said. 'He is just a fool. And a messenger,' she added lightly, and stretched over me to pour the tea.

Percy *was* to be a messenger, of course. I had realised that the previous night, or at least I had suspected it. He would be released and he would take this story back to the Pink 'Un, and to Mary, probably with a copy of the photograph which had just been taken.

The tea was hot and good. I felt better for it.

'You'll want a bath, I suppose,' said Elsa. 'Oh, it's quite late, but we obey the blackout and have shutters.' She laughed again, and added: 'Will you take them down?'

I found that I was wearing borrowed pyjamas, and saw

75

a man's dressing-gown draped over the back of a chair. I put this on, pushed my hands through my hair, and took down the shutters which fitted inside the window. Not until the daylight poured into the room, and I saw the sun shining on the front lawn and the garden gates, did I realise why she had asked me to take down the blackout.

I stared into a front garden, *which was entirely different from the garden of the house at Staines!*

·　　　·　　　·　　　·　　　·

The thick hedge which had hidden the other road from sight was gone, and in its place was a tall fence, part of it newly creosoted. Where there had been yew hedges on other sides of the garden, here there were cypresses. The trees, the flower beds and the lawns were different; so was a background of wooded hills.

I tried to show no expression as I turned from the window, and sat down in an easy chair facing Elsa. She had a pleasant, human smile—as if she were trying to show me that she had two personalities. I believe that to be true.

'Was that such a shock?' she asked.

'I'm getting used to the unexpected,' I replied.

'Bruce,' said Elsa Bruenning, standing up from her bed and walking towards me, 'you weren't born to be on the losing side. You *can't* win against the Baron, and by now you should realise that. Join him. Don't wait until he loses patience and orders your execution.'

The last word sounded cold and ugly.

'Why should you be so interested?' I asked her.

'You are very different from the man I expected,' she said, sitting on the arm of my chair. 'You and I could have much in common.'

I moistened my lips.

'Are you aware that I was to have been married shortly?'

'Yes. I know when, where, and to whom.' She forced my

76

head round so that I had to look into her eyes. 'Now understand this,' she went on, with an underlying note of savagery in her voice. 'Photographs were taken, and the woman Dell will see them. Your man will be released and he will talk—how he will talk! That was why he was brought here, why he had instructions to bring tea. But he is not to be released yet.'

'It doesn't seem to matter when,' I said, but my heart began to thump.

'It makes a great deal of difference,' replied Elsa. 'Until he gets away he can say nothing. We need him only to use as evidence against you. If you obey the instructions of the Baron, Briggs need not tell his story, and the photographs need never be shown.'

'None of this seems to be making sense,' I complained.

'It makes good sense,' said Elsa lightly. 'You don't have to understand all of it, that can be safely left to the Baron. You have to undertake to do whatever he wants, and you will be quite safe, and within limits free.'

'Oh, it's madness.' I cried. 'I've worked for Sir Robert Holt for years. I am engaged to his leading agent. And this is my country . . .'

'A *dead* country,' she interpolated.

Of course, she believed that.

The years of Nazi progress with virtually no opposition, those terrible wasted years when democracy had betrayed itself and all its friends, when there had been neither power nor courage nor faith in England, had taken their toll. Even when Britain had fought back, the tragedy of Norway showed her half-hearted and unprepared.

But Elsa Bruenning believed that we were a dead race, ready for the domination of the German Reich.

I came near to laughing in her face, telling her that whatever they did to me their time in England was short; that it would not be long before there was yet another fugitive

77

from the Wilhelmstrasse, a fugitive from the wrath and bitterness of a deluded German people.

Instead, I turned my face away.

'I can't betray them,' I muttered.

'*They* are the betrayers,' Elsa declared. 'The people who do not know what is good for the world.'

She stopped.

That was the first time that I learned how the Withered Man affected her, and in fact all of those who worked for him. I had imagined that only I, or those likely to suffer from his ruthless brutality, knew the momentary panic that came when hearing his approach. Instead, she turned her head towards the door, and drew in a sharp breath.

Not far away came: *Thump. A pause. Thump—thump —thump.*

I sprang to my feet, almost pushing her from the arm of the chair, wishing desperately that I could close my ears to von Horssell's approach. Instead I lit a cigarette. The thumping grew louder until it stopped outside the door, and the handle began to turn.

Slowly and impassively, von Horssell entered. He carried an envelope under his withered arm, and when he had reached me, tapped this with his left hand. I took the envelope and opened it. The contents should not have surprised me, but they did.

The flashlight photographs had already been developed, and here were prints. There was no mistaking Elsa, nor me—as she kissed me. Involuntarily, too, my arm had gone about her shoulders. It was a damnable indictment.

But it was not all.

There was a gramophone record, and before I could do anything with it Elsa stepped up, took it from me, and then set it on a small gramophone which was against the dressing-table. The thoroughness of everything they did was the most frightening thing about them.

The needle scratched noisily, and then I heard Cator's

78

rough voice. A moment later there was a scuffle, followed by Percy Briggs threatening to squeeze his throat. My own voice followed.

I listened through a nightmare of the conversation between Percy and me. I had aimed to destroy Percy's faith in my loyalty, and I had talked far more effectively than I had dreamed.

Von Horssell's queer light eyes stared unwinkingly at me, and there was an undertone of his heavy breathing. When the speaking finished and Elsa stopped the gramophone, he said:

'I am going to try you out, Murdoch. You vill go from here and continue—ostensibly—to vork for Holt. From time to time you vill report to me of all der things of importance. If there is reason for me to believe that you lie—*ach*, der photographs and der record vill be sent to Holt, and Briggs will be released to tell of vot he saw this morning. You understand all that it means?'

'I understand,' I said dully.

'Dat iss good. And now . . .' He looked behind me, towards Elsa, and she took something from the dressing-table drawer. 'Look at these while you dress, Murdoch. You vill understand from them vot happens to those who betray *me*.'

I took the photographs Elsa handed me, and stared at them. I did not hear von Horssell nor Elsa go out, I was so torn by the horror of the mutilated creatures in those photographs, men who had been subjected to such horrors of maltreatment and torture that my stomach heaved.

II

Clean Air

My clothes, newly pressed, were in the wardrobe, and my shoes were by its side. Shaving gear was on the dressing-table, and the water from a tap of the hand-basin in a corner of the room ran hot. I lost no time in dressing, and the appalling efficiency of that household had a further demonstration when, as I was putting on my coat, the door opened and a manservant I had not seen before brought in a laden breakfast tray. I did not expect to want much breakfast, but the bacon, eggs and tomatoes were plentiful, the toast crisp, and the butter creamy. I enjoyed the meal.

Obviously I was to be released.

There should be no difficulty in telling Holt and Mary just what I was doing. I was sure that I had done the only thing possible. But it was a brittle kind of satisfaction.

The door opened again, and Cator took me downstairs.

The narrow passage outside my room ended in a heavy door which opened automatically when Cator pressed a button. On the other side of the door the passage widened, and to all appearances there was nothing beyond it. I smelt disinfectant, but thought that I was imagining it until I saw a nurse in white uniform entering a door on the right.

The stairs were covered with rubber.

Into a room leading from the main hall I went at Cator's growled order.

Von Horssell was sitting in a long chair, with his withered leg on a stoool, and his ebony stick nearby. Elsa was not present. The Baron was writing in a small notebook, and he ignored me until he had finished. Then he looked up.

'Your instructions vill reach you, Murdoch, ven you arrive in London. For the time being, you vill remember all I haff said—and also you vill remember that if there iss reason for me to believe you are playing against me—then Briggs vill get der treatment given to the men you saw in der photographs.'

Percy!

I had forgotten that, forgotten the full implications of his presence. I do not know whether I showed my feelings as I tried to keep poker-faced. Von Horssell nodded, then looked away. He gave me the impression that I was a very small cog in his wheel.

'I vill see you another time,' he grunted.

'Come on,' said Cator.

I followed him out, and this time I saw two more nurses, and a man being brought into the hall on a stretcher. I realised that ostensibly this was a nursing-home, and that von Horssell used that as a cover.

'Put these on,' ordered Cator.

'These' were a pair of glasses, with dark lenses and side-pieces, not unlike the goggles which an oxy-acetylene welder uses.

When they were on I could see nothing, and Cator fastened them behind my head. In a state of darkness I was led out, and again I realised the full cunning of it. No one would be surprised at seeing a man with blue glasses being led from a nursing-home.

I was bundled into a car, and Cator climbed in with me; I had a feeling that he would not be loath to shoot me. Nothing happened, however, and the car made a good speed after several miles of slow progress and many stops. I kept my ears wide open, trying to recognise sounds which might help me to identify the place later, but nothing came.

The car slowed down after about an hour, and Cator took off the glasses. Brilliant sunlight dazzled my eyes, and when I could see clearly again Cator and the other car were moving away, while a Lagonda stood in the roadside within a yard of me.

It was my own car!

At least I acted swiftly now. There was a pair of binoculars in the dashboard pocket, and I took them out. Peering through them I could not only see the make of Cator's car, a small Morris, but also the number.

I was in a wide main road with traffic passing in all directions. Not far ahead was a thirty-mile limit sign, and I climbed into the Lagonda and drove towards the village. It was a pleasant place, with a green and a pond, and ducks swimming idly on the clear water. I was less interested in ducks than in a telephone kiosk nearby.

I drew up outside it and called the Exchange.

'I want Sloane 81812,' I said urgently, 'and the charges will be reversed. Hurry it for me, please.'

'Sloane 81812,' a girl repeated, and the line went dead for a moment. Then she came back. 'Is that a London number?'

'Yes.'

The disc in the telephone told me that I was in the area covered by Ringwood. I had been brought nearly a hundred miles from Staines. I saw the post office opposite the kiosk, and read:

Burley Green P.O.

Burley Green, not far from Ringwood—that meant that I was within a few miles of the place where Mick and Denyer had started to look for the suspect refugees. Whatever else, we were better off. I had a full description of von Horssell and of Elsa, Cator and some of the servants.

I heard the clang of the telephone being lifted at the other end, and the girl on the Exchange asking whether the call charge would be met by the London subscriber. I felt a sharp relief when I heard Pinky's testy voice.

'Yes, yes, put him through.'

I knew then how remote had seemed the chance of speaking to Pinky again.

'Pinky . . .' I began.

'And where—the—devil have—*you* been?' bellowed Pinky, so loudly that I snatched the receiver from my ear. 'I've got half the country looking for you, and . . .'

'Let me get a word in!' I protested. 'I'm at Ringwood. Will you have a call put out for a Morris 10, Number 1BOU23, which started north from here about ten minutes ago. Have it followed, and not by police cars, but by a vehicle that won't be suspect.'

There was a pause before Pinky said: 'Wait a minute.'

I heard him speaking into another telephone, and knew that not a second would be lost. There was a chance that Cator would be picked up, and that the nursing-home would be located.

Pinky soon came back on the line.

'All right, that's done. Anything else?'

'Did you get any word from Mick or Denyer?' I demanded.

'We got two or three, yes,' said Pinky. 'Mick and Ted are waiting for you in London. Mary, too. My God, Bruce, you scared us! Did you have to keep us waiting for two days?'

I gasped: '*What!*'

'Don't bellow in my ear!' shouted Pinky irascibly. 'You heard what I said—oh, well, don't waste time now but come up here and report at once. Briggs all right?'

That question came like a douche of cold water.

'No,' I said, 'Percy is anything but all right. Listen, Pinky. I shall be followed. I expect these people know that I'm often at Sloane Square, and I'd better meet you somewhere else, we don't want to give anything else away.'

'All right,' grunted Pinky. 'Your flat.'

The news that I had been missing for two days had an effect like a delayed-action bomb. I could have sworn that I had gone to sleep one night and awakened the next morning.

Yet this, according to Pinky, was the *third* morning.

I hurried back to the Lagonda, but the shocks were not finished yet. For on the driving-seat of the car was a small slip of paper, bearing the printed letters:

Remember Briggs

And on the seat next to the driver's was a photograph, face downwards, of one of those mutilated victims of the Withered Man.

.   .   .   .   ʼ

I insisted on telling the whole story to Pinky alone.

He was a better judge of how much the others should know, although of course I would expect Mary to know everything that mattered, especially as far as Elsa was concerned. Pinky sprawled back in an easy chair in my bedroom, while the others stayed in the lounge. They—particularly Ted and Mick—were probably cursing me, but they had cursed me before.

Pinky's pink countenance was as smooth and shiny as a child's. Only his eyes looked grave. From time to time he nodded, then scribbled in a notebook that he carried about with him. When at last I finished, he said:

'Well, it could be worse, and it could be a lot better. Briggs is worse off than any of us, of course.' He sighed. 'Oh, well, damn-and-blast the lot of 'em. They're stronger than I thought.'

It would not have surprised me had Pinky been jubilant about the development. After all, there was a reasonable chance of keeping me indefinitely in von Horssell's camp, until the time came for striking a blow that might smash not only the Withered Man but the greater part of the Fifth

Column activities. I felt a sharp rise of irritation.

'They're not as strong as all that.'

Pinky looked at me oddly.

'No?' His voice was surprisingly gentle. 'I wish I thought so. There was a violent air-raid on an East Coast town last night. Orders were given for the sirens, but none sounded. The casualties were doubled if not trebled because the bombs started to fall before anyone took cover.'

I felt cold.

'Sabotage?'

'Cancelled orders,' Pinky said savagely. 'Telephone wires cut. The whole range of the Withered Man's operations carried out as effectively as in Holland. I—oh, well,' he added, and he grinned although it was not his normal confident beam. 'We'll face it. What are your ideas?'

'Is there any word of that Morris 10?'

'No.'

'Has anything else happened like the business last night?'

'A Local Defence Volunteer commander was assassinated,' Pinky grunted. 'A petrol store in East Anglia was burned out. A small factory turning out gas-masks was ruined by an explosion—presumed accidental, probably Fifth Columnist. Thing is,' he went on fiercely, 'it is absolutely essential to get at the head of them, and von Horssell is the head. I'm not surprised. I knew he was busy somewhere, and he has the cunning of von Rintelen with the mercilessness of Hess. But—he might be anywhere.'

'Damn it,' I said, 'there's no need to be defeatist. We might get him at the place I left this morning.' As I spoke I realised that Pinky was talking in much the same way as I had spoken to Percy. I remembered, too, that I had been acting.

Now Pinky is as sublime an actor as any I know.

But Mary and I have usually been able to see beneath the surface, and we have never known Pinky really defeatist. I did not think he was then. But for some reason I could not fathom but which worried me, he wanted me to believe that he was losing hope.

I had wanted Percy to believe that.

And then Pinky took my breath away.

'Murdoch,' he said—and he had not used my surname for two years, except when others had been present. 'I don't like the present situation. I think you're tired, like the others. I want you to take the rest you were talking about earlier in the week.'

I was hardly able to believe my ears.

'But . . .' I began.

'Don't argue!' snapped Pinky, but there was nothing of his normal irascibility in his attitude; he was serious, and he was also my commanding officer. 'You're relieved from duty for the next seven days.' He stood up and pushed his chair back, looked at me expressionlessly, and then went out of the room.

There was a fog in my mind thicker than when I had been drugged by von Horssell, but there was something worse. Then I had been worried, and scared, but I had not been *hurt*. I realise now that the emotion was of hurt, of sick, incredible pain because I felt that the trust which Pinky had imposed in me for years was gone.

I must have been in the room, alone, for five minutes. Then, more wearily than I have moved for a long time, I went into the lounge. It was empty. I stepped to the window, and looked out.

Pinky was stepping into a Daimler car, and a chauffeur was standing by the open door. From that height it was difficult to be sure of anything, but I caught my breath, for the chauffeur *looked* like Percival Briggs. I flung the window up and craned my neck.

It *was* Percy.

Angell and Fuller were standing on the pavement by the car, and they climbed in past the Cockney. I was very close to throwing myself out of that window. It was so increasingly obvious what had happened. Percy had escaped, might even have been released. In some diabolical way von Horssell had contrived to destroy *Pinky's* faith in me.

And yet there had been no suggestion of that on the telephone, while it seemed to defeat his own ends.

Ted's attitude, and Mick's, had been genuine enough when I had returned.

Mary . . .

Mary had looked harassed and worried, and had clung to me as though I was leaving on a perilous mission instead of returning from one.

I moved to the dining-room, wondering if I should find her there, but she was missing. I was alone in the flat, and alone with thoughts which were hideous. I was suspect by my own Chief, by my friends, by the woman I loved as I had not known love was possible.

Pinky must be made to believe me!

I withdrew my head quickly, and almost missed what started to happen down below. I caught a glimpse of a Lancia coming from the Marble Arch direction towards Pinky's Daimler. Its driver swung his wheel, and crashed broadside into the larger car.

12

Meeting in Streatham

This was a deliberate effort to smash Pinky and other members of S.1, and I completely forgot my own troubles in a desperate fear for my leader. I swung from the window and reached the door in a few strides. The crash of the collision still echoed in my ears, and I could hear the screeching of brakes from the street, the shrill cry of a police whistle.

I wrenched the door open—and stopped. Elsa stood in the threshold of the doorway opposite.

I had not known that the flat was occupied. Like many in Central London the block had been practically deserted when the raids had first started.

Elsa was dressed in a silk blouse and a tweed skirt, and she looked lovely; cool, calm and serene. She was smiling, her teeth just showing and her eyes mocking. I stood still, and she moved towards me, closing her door behind her. I went back into the lounge-hall.

'Worried?' she said.

'I've just seen my friends smashed up,' I growled. 'If you think I enjoy that . . .' I did not finish.

'Individuals count for nothing, Bruce. You heard what Holt said to you—you've been retired. Are you blind to what that means?'

I muttered: 'It means that he's doubtful whether I'm reliable.'

'We made sure he's *very* doubtful.'

'But it's all so damned silly! What good am I to you if Holt suspects? He wouldn't have done had you let me play my own game!'

'Your own game was a peculiar one. But you see we had taken it for granted that you would not change sides so quickly or so easily. You acted very well, I'll admit. In fact Cator and others were quite sure that you could be relied on to do what we wanted. But I doubted it, and the Baron is very thorough—you know that.'

'I still don't see what you're driving at.'

'Your very dull,' said Elsa, and there was a touch of contempt in her voice which stung. 'Holt isn't certain of you any longer. He doesn't want to have you arrested, doesn't want to think his leading agent has been persuaded to change sides, but he's not *sure*.'

I said: 'I see.'

The very essence of Fifth Column work was to create uncertainty among the people *and* the organisations. To make A.R.P. workers wonder whether their leaders could be relied on, to make the personnel of the volunteer forces wonder if there was treachery at the head. To plant doubts in every mind as to the ability of the Government to withstand the Hitler onslaught.

And they had made Pinky uncertain of me.

He would wonder which others could be relied on, and he would have me watched closely. If I made a 'false' step I would be in danger of arrest from my own people.

'You *can't* win, Bruce,' she said. 'Even this morning, within the last five minutes, that car was crashed. Holt might not be hurt, but he will be aware of the danger every living minute. Institutions you thought were inviolate are being undermined. Members of Parliament have been arrested, political party leaders are detained, *but for every one arrested a dozen are free and working for the Fatherland*. You could move among a thousand men, and yet not be *sure* of any one of them. You moved into this flat because Holt knew your other flat was watched and the telephone lines were tapped. This one is watched, too. I heard *all* of your conversation. A record of it is on its way to the Baron. It's too big for you, too thorough!'

That was when I wanted to laugh. By her very thoroughness she had been outwitted; and the Pink 'Un had outwitted me.

He had known that she had been listening!

He had acted just as I had done with Percy, simply to give von Horssell further evidence that I was suspect, and therefore good material for von Horssell to work on.

'All right, you win,' I said dejectedly. 'Where do I go now?'

I could see that she was pleased.

'Number 8, Clarkville Road, Streatham,' she said. 'Be

89

there at seven-thirty tonight, and make sure that you are not followed. But'—she had started to walk to the door, but then swung round on me fiercely—'don't change your mind again. One more mistake and you'll be killed.'

She went out while I turned that address over and over in my mind.

8 Clarkville Road, Streatham.

I was to be there at half-past seven.

.   .   .   .

After Elsa had gone I looked out of the window in time to see Pinky and the others as a car came up and drove off with them: none of them seemed to be hurt. There was no sign of Mary. The Lancia had been crushed by the collision, and was on its side. A Black Maria was going towards Marble Arch, presumably with the driver of the Lancia and any passengers in it.

There were moments when I was quite sure that I was right in imagining that Pinky had put up a colossal bluff, others when doubts assailed me. Twice I lifted the telephone, intending to call the Sloane Square office, and each time I resisted the temptation.

I did ring Mary's flat, a small one in Shepherd Market. There was no answer to my ringing, however.

Towards six o'clock the sirens wailed and soon afterwards I heard the droning of aircraft. An occasional *crash* of an A.A. gun added to the noise, and I saw a flight of Hurricanes chasing a Junkers 88 across the blue sky. Through the closed windows, criss-crossed with gummed paper, I looked out on the streets and the Park. The crowds of people on their way home from work, or sunning themselves in the tree-lined gardens, went in orderly fashion towards the A.R.P. trenches, where queues formed. A few people donned gas-masks. A.R.P. cars patrolled Park Lane, while the A.A. fire grew more intense and set the pictures on the walls quivering, crockery in the kitchen shaking and jingling.

An extra loud *crump!* told of a bomb not far away, and I heard glass smashing. I took that as a signal to get away from the window, and went into Percy's bedroom, which had been turned into the temporary shelter.

The raid lasted little more than twenty minutes. Soon, the crowds were thronging the streets again, and traffic crowded the road.

There was nothing in the larder, and I rang for a snack from the restaurant. I finished soon after seven o'clock, then examined a map of S.W. London. I found Clarkville Road just off Tooting Bec Road, and soon after seven started off in the Lagonda.

By force of habit I looked round from time to time but I did not appear to be followed.

The trouble was—*I could not be sure*.

I reached 8, Clarkville Road just after seven-thirty. It was a large house, standing in its own grounds. I was admitted by a little man who looked at me carefully, and demanded to see my English Registration Card, not anything from von Horssell.

There was much mystery about the way I was shown through three empty rooms, questioned and stopped each time. It seemed senseless, but it happened. The attendants in each case were men.

I went up a wide flight of stairs, and was ushered by a woman into a large room which in normal times might have been a ballroom. There were wooden seats and forms across the middle of the room, and a raised platform at one end.

Fifty or sixty people were present.

There was a hum of conversation, but what amazed me most was the fact that many of the men—only a sprinkling of women was present—might have been seen in any Berlin *bierhaus*. Clipped hair, monocles, the glassy stare of the Prussian.

Here and there I heard a smatter of German, sometimes of French. A dozen times newcomers entered, using the Hitler salute so automatically that I knew they were accustomed to it. Thousands of aliens had been arrested but hardly an Englishman was present.

A squint-eyed man next to me leaned forward and muttered:

'It iss not vise, friend.'

'No?' I said, making it a question.

He stared, probably surprised by my lack of accent.

'Der are too many of us here,' he muttered. 'If der poliss should come—it is finish.'

I said slowly: '*He* knows what he is doing.'

'*Ja*—it has always been,' admitted the other, and he seemed satisfied. I was not. I did not know whether to expect von Horssell to address the meeting in person, and I looked in vain for Elsa or for anyone I had seen at the Staines house.

The room was now so full that at least a hundred and fifty people were present; some wert standing in the gangways. It grew hot and smoky, and only a few windows were open an inch or so.

At last I saw someone come through.

An undersized man, incredibly wrinkled, with a monocle dangling from his lapel, stepped smartly to the dais, reached it, and raised a hand in the Nazi salute. Mine went up automatically—as did all the others. There was no 'Heil Hitler', but before the man started to speak attendants closed all the windows. There appeared to be no means of ventilation, but electric fans were moving at speed and causing a faint hum as a background to the conversation. This stopped, and the man on my left leaned forward.

'*Donnerwetter*, vot use is Loebbels? He talks, talks, talks! Action, dat iss needed, my friendt, action fast!'

'It will come,' I said.

It was incredible that such a sentiment could be uttered in London over a year after the beginning of the war. Incredible that this gathering of Germans or pro-Germans could take place in a thickly populated district within a stone's throw—more or less—of the hub of Allied activities.

The little man called Loebbels began to talk.

He had a high-pitched voice and spluttered when he shouted his words, his lips turned back and showed the gums beneath his teeth. He waved his scraggy little arms about and shook his fists towards the ceiling. He raved against the British Government and the 'tyranny' of British Imperialism. He listed a dozen 'atrocities', all lies which had been nailed months before. He gave a violent diatribe against organised justice and mercy, and I was sick at the thought of so much beastliness, so much barbarism.

Loebbels worked himself up to a great pitch of frenzy, *but he had the meeting with him!*

Even the squinting man was gazing in rapt attention at Loebbels, and all other eyes seemed to be staring towards the speaker. There were expressions of incredible cruelty, of sheer sadistic lust, on some faces. On others there was a rabid fanaticism which gave voice to itself in a low-throated growl when Loebbels stopped in the midddle of a sentence, and yelled:

'Who vill end all this? Who, who, who?'

'*Heil*, Hitler!'

Easy to understand, then, why the windows had been closed. Easy to know why it was imperative that no sound reach the street outside.

Loebbels flung both hands outwards.

'The Führer,' he bellowed, and I saw that he was drooling at the lips. 'The All Highest, Adolf Hitler, saviour of the mighty Aryan race, appointed ruler of the world, divine . . .'

Crash!

The noise stopped even Loebbels, jerked everyone out of the trance into which he had worked them. It came again:

Crash!

'Der poliss!' gasped the squint-eyed man at my side. 'I knew it vould come, I knew!'

There was a wild scramble now for the door at the far end of the room. Loebbels jumped from the platform like a lizard, and streaked for the door. The banging at the door near me increased, and then suddenly it opened. A dozen police were there, most of them armed. At the same moment the far door was broken, and Loebbels was pushed back with the mob which had followed him.

I thought that there would be a general mêlée. A man near me drew a gun, and I leaned across the squinting man and struck it aside. As I did so a hefty man in blue passed me, and his truncheon descended on the would-be gunman's neck.

That proved enough.

The fanatical crowd was silent and frightened. A woman whose voice had screeched louder than the others with her 'Heil Hitler!' had fainted.

I stood and watched as if from a long distance off. It had not struck home that I was one of the crowd—one of the meeting whose avowed object had been the striking at vital points in England. Not until a policeman gripped my shoulder and urged me towards the door did I realise that.

Protest was useless.

There was a string of covered lorries outside, and the prisoners were bundled into them. I was in the third of six lorries, with twenty or thirty people, all standing. We swayed heavily against each other as it turned a corner.

'Vere vill dey take us?' a man asked.

'Brixton Prison, probably,' I heard myself saying.

'*Ach*, I knew it, I knew it,' moaned the squinting man,

who had stuck close to me all the time. 'Loebbels, he iss der vool, alvays der vool!'

'Shut up, there!' This from one of three policemen with rifles, standing at the back of the oorry. Crowds stared at us from the streets as we went along, and at one place where the lorries were forced to slow down there were angry shouts from a crowd which had gathered quickly.

'*Kill the dirty swine!*'

'*Swing the Huns!*'

Someone started pelting the inside of the lorry with tomatoes and fruit from a nearby greengrocer's. I was lucky —an apple stung my forehead, but did no damage. Most of the others were plastered with tomato and orange juice before we moved off. I thought with a twinge of ironic humour that it was typical of an English crowd to shout for blood and to throw soft fruit.

We did not go to Brixton.

It was getting dusk, but I recognised the Great West Road, and knew that once again I was on the way to Staines. We did not go through the river town, however, but kept along the Bath Road and, just before reaching Slough, turned right. In a short while we were slowing down outside an internment camp where guards with fixed bayonets stood at intervals along the barricaded encampment. The gates were opened and the lorries went lumbering through.

We entered a wooden building in single file.

Inside, the women were sent in one direction, the men in another. A long, bare room housed us for a few minutes, but one by one we were taken into a small ante-room. When I went in I was searched quickly yet thoroughly, and although I was treated roughly there was a certain clumsy courtesy in the way I was handled.

A young lieutenant looked at me.

'*You're* not the type,' he said. 'Scottish, aren't you?'

'Scottish,' I agreed.

'My God!' he said. 'All right, get on with you. Behave yourself, and you won't have anything to grumble about.'

'*Yer ruddy well ought ter 'ave*,' muttered a grey-haired sergeant, *sotto voce*. He aided my progress into yet another room with a surreptitious knee in the rear.

For the first time since leaving the flat I was on my own.

It was only for a moment, and then two soldiers joined me and I was marched off between them. I was taken out of the big shed and through the fast gathering gloom led to another. I was near the door of it when I saw a little party of soldiers standing at ease nearby.

And, in the familiar khaki, I saw the unmistakable face and figure of von Horssell's man, Meltze!

13

I am Warned

Meltze, among the uniformed guards of the encampment which probably housed a thousand or more enemy aliens!

I had no time to speak, and even had I wanted to, doubted whether my guards would have been willing. I entered another, smaller shed, filled with nausea, but I had little time then to concentrate on that, for I found myself in a small room where three men sat on the far side of a large desk. All three were in uniform, but I had another shock.

The middle of the trio was Sir Robert Holt, O.B.E.

He had his cap pushed to the back of his head, and the front of his bald cranium showed. His eyes were twinkling in a very different expression from what I had seen earlier that day.

' 'Lo, Bruce,' he said, and all the doubts and uncertain-

ties I had possessed earlier disappeared. I have never been
so grateful for a 'Bruce'.

'Well, well,' I said weakly. 'You.'

'Sorry and all that,' said the Pink 'Un. 'Had to do it—
no need to worry you about that now, what you can't guess
you can learn afterwards. You're going into solitary confinement. So are a dozen others. In a day, or less, you'll be
released. Once outside, you'll "escape". Follow?'

'Yes,' I said breathlessly.

'Von H. will pick you up,' said Pinky. 'It's all being
arranged. Throw hate in plenty. Curse me to your heart's
content.' Pinky grinned. 'Link up with von H. and do what
he tells you unless it's anything of vital importance. For
anything like that get word through to me at S.S.'

Sloane Square, of course. 'Yes,' I said.

'Briggs still thinks it's genuine,' said Pinky, and I thought
he hesitated for a moment. 'So does Mary, And the others.
You're on your own. Got that, Bruce?'

'Yes,' I said, more stiffly. A picture of Mary was in my
mind's eye.

'I've done all I could to prove the case against you,'
Pinky said. 'They're *all* being watched by von H. Not
approached, just watched. They're overheard, and their
feelings are judged pretty soundly. We've half a dozen of
the Columnists working with us—oh, I know them. Von
H. doesn't think I do, but I know them all right. Listening,
Bruce?'

'Of course.'

'Good!' Pinky lifted a plump hand. 'Listen hard. All
this that's happened so far is negligible. Von H. is playing
for something big, something to coincide with a major
effort to overrun us. *That's* your job. Find what it is. I can
stop the small stuff, or most of it, but I must know what he's
planning for the *blitzkrieg* over here. I should say the next
attempt at one,' grunted Pinky. 'I'm not taking any chance,
Bruce. I'm putting all my trust in you, on this angle. I've

97

had Mary, Ted and Mick working on others. If you contact with them and it's necessary for you to prove you're with us, the word is . . .' He leaned forward, and I did likewise, while the two officers on either side of him sat like dummies and stared ahead of them.

'*Rumcattel*,' whispered Pinky hoarsely. 'No, it doesn't make sense, but it's the word they're using now—one I gave them this afternoon, and which you couldn't use unless you'd seen me since. Use it only in real emergency. By that,' added Pinky more loudly, 'I mean something more than a personal one. Use it only if you can't avoid it.' He whispered again: 'Rumcattel. Got it?'

'Yes.'

'All right,' said Pinky, and then he roared: 'All right, off with you! Next one, guards!'

I leaned forward and said urgently: 'Pinky—one of von H.'s men is in uniform outside.'

Pinky stared.

'*What!*'

'It's true,' I snapped. 'It . . .'

And then I stopped.

Whether I could have done anything to prevent what followed by talking of Meltze earlier I don't know. I shall always believe that I could, and that in a measure I was responsible for the tragedies of that night. But Pinky and others assure me that it was quite impossible in the time at his disposal, even had 'Meltze' been the first word I had uttered.

The first thing was the wail of sirens, for the encampment was fitted with them. They rose and fell with feverish inconsistency, but as they stopped I could hear the roar of aero-engines, and I detected the deep throbbing note of the Dornier. Before Pinky had risen to his feet there came:

Crump! Crump-crump-crump! from bombs falling nearby. I made an instinctive movement to my helmet, which I was so used to carrying, but it was not there of course. Pinky and the others made for a small door, and my guards urged me in his wake. As I reached the door there was an explosion so close that it sent débris hurtling against the wooden walls of the shed. Some of the boards caved in, and a piece of metal hurtled right through to the other side.

Crump—crump—crump!

I distinctly heard Pinky say:

'Oh, damn! And I'm in a hurry.'

What else he said was drowned, but not in the thudding of high explosive bombs alone. Mingled with their sound was the *rat-tat-tat* of machine-guns. At first they were so close that I thought the raiders must be within fifty or so feet of the roof, but I was quick to realise that the droning of the engines was much further away.

The machine-guns were in action on the ground.

Attacking the beggars, I thought.

But I was wrong—dreadfully wrong.

I first knew it when Pinky opened the door, and then darted back. At the same moment there was a burst of machine-gun fire not fifty feet away from the shed, and bullets swept through the open door, and bit their way through the wood of the walls. I heard one of the guards gasp, and I flung myself as close to the far wall as I could get.

Pinky was on his hands and knees. His hat had fallen, and his pink face looked startled.

Then we heard the engines of lorries starting up.

I knew what was happening then. I think I had known from the time I had realised that the machine-guns were not only in action on the ground, but were being used *against* the authorities. At all events, lorry after lorry started up, and I could hear them sweeping through the open gates.

There were five in all.

Slowly the sound of their engines died away, while the sound of machine-gunning had stopped. Orders were being shouted, and other engines started up, but before anything moved in pursuit the drone of the bombers came from directly above us again, and the deadly *crump-crump-crump* began. I could see the fiery bursts of the explosions, see the billow of smoke and débris as it went upwards and outwards.

I hugged the floor and the wall.

It was intense while it lasted, but that was not for no more than sixty seconds. My ears ringing and my legs unsteady, I straightened up.

I heard cries from the wounded, and saw flashlights being used. The regular roar of the A.A. guns had been going on all the time—I found it so much to be expected that I was almost oblivious to it. Behind the hut was a network of searchlights, and a Dornier was caught in the beam of one. A dozen others switched towards it, and puffs of smoke chased it.

One shell hit its target.

I knew it when I saw the smoke and flame spreading out, wider by far than from any individual burst. And then the machine toppled over and, afire at both ends, fell in a blazing line of fire which lit up the heavens.

Fighters were chasing across the skies in pursuit of the other bombers, and I breathed with relief. But it was short-lived, for a soldier grabbed my arm.

'No, *you* don't!'

He was one of the men who had heard Pinky, and he should have known better—or I thought so at first. Then, not far from me and staring my way, I saw Meltze.

I knew then that Pinky wasn't taking any chances.

. . . . .

I had no objection to my twenty-four hours of solitary confinement. The food was only fair, but it was plentiful and I was given some books—Pinky had been behind that, for among them was *Nemesis*, Douglas Reed's book which I had not had time to read. I shall always believe that Reed was the first journalist to write a book which showed clearly and without any shadow of doubt that we were wrong in dealing with Hitler, or even trying to.

I had no idea how many casualties there had been the previous night, but when I was taken for a short walk round the parade ground—on my own but for two guards—I saw some of the débris. One hut had been smashed completely, and the wreckage of a lorry was on its side, but drawn out of the roadway. Other huts were badly damaged.

But for that brief talk with Pinky I would have been a badly worried man, and not because of my own plight.

Von Horssell had arranged it all, of course. The capture of his Fifth Columnists had probably been known, and the preparations for the raid in Streatham learned beforehand. It *must* have been done that way, for von Horssell had to get word to France or Belgium—or Holland—for the bombing squadron to come over.

Thoroughness—unrelieved and almost frightening.

The capture of a hundred and fifty spies and traitors, followed by a bombing raid which had coincided with the arrival at the encampment. Men actually at the encampment ready to start the gunning, and then to stop the guards from organising themselves and preventing the escape of most of the prisoners. Another raid, to stop pursuit.

It was German all over.

And in a large measure it had succeded.

I was halfway through *Nemesis* when my evening meal was brought in. As usual, there was a guard and an orderly with it. I looked up at the guard, and I had a job to stop from exclaiming.

It was Meltze.

Almost imperceptibly he nodded, and then glanced towards the food. I winked just enough for him to see it, and then the orderly went out of the small wooden shed. I explored among the sandwiches for a message, and I found it.

On the outside of a thin slip of folded paper was the pencilled drawing of a wheel-chair.

I opened the paper quickly, and read:

You will be exercised at dusk. Make for the gate marked with a red cross. The guard's rifle will be loaded with blanks. A car will pick you up. Destroy this.

I was less appalled by the fact that von Horssell could make those arrangements—for Pinky had not only known it, but had forestalled it. I had cigarettes and matches, and was able to burn the note.

My door was unlocked at last and I was taken out by a guard who clearly had little time for me. He was a Cockney with a fine control of Billingsgate epithet. I don't blame him for using it.

It did not take me long to see the gate marked with a red cross. It was heavily protected with barbed wire, but when I reached the parade ground it was not guarded, although there was a sentry box nearby. I walked towards it casually, and for some seconds stood against the barbed wire and looked into the fields beyond.

The guard growled: 'Pick your feet up. You're exercisin', not sleepin'!'

I swung round on him with apparent anger.

'Carry out your instructions—don't exceed them!'

He glared, and I think he would have enjoyed prodding me with his bayonet.

'None o' *your* lip, you bloody traitor! I was told to keep you walkin'—keep to it!'

I moved towards the gate, and he was very near me. I stopped suddenly and looked down at the ground. He did the same—and I back-heeled.

He gasped and went sprawling, for there had been a

lot of power behind that kick. But I forgot him as I rushed for the gate. I had a moment of fear that it would be locked, but it opened at a touch—the staff work had been perfect. I was already outside when I heard the first *crack!* from behind me. I experienced another moment of panic lest the bullets should be real ones and not blanks, but nothing hit me, nor the ground near me. I heard the roar of a car engine, and then a bugle, followed by several sharp blasts on a siren.

The car was coming from distant trees.

I recognised Elsa as it came towards me. She was in the back, but leaning forward so that her face was nearly on a level with Cator's. Cator was at the wheel.

I knew what to expect.

The car slowed down, and the steel shutters disappeared. We were near a small garage on the outskirts of Slough, and another car pulled out as we approached. I jumped out, and Elsa followed me, with Cator bringing up the rear. The garage man nodded, and I made a note of the name— the *Five Star Garage, Slough*—for that needed to be raided at the earliest possible moment.

The second car was an old Buick.

There was a noticeable easing of the tension after we had gone half a mile, and Elsa deigned to notice me. She turned, and I saw her half-mocking, half-savage smile.

'Well,' she said, 'we did it for you, Bruce.'

'Well,' I grunted, 'you got me into it.'

She opened her mouth and laughed.

'Gratitude, my friend! Do you know that you were for a court martial tonight? That you would have been shot tomorrow morning?'

I licked my lips.

'I—I didn't realise it.'

'Well, you can realise it now,' she said, and again the note of savagery was pronounced. 'They want you, *dead or alive*, Murdoch. Your own people—and the one way to escape is to do everything Baron von Horssell tells you.'

I said bitterly: 'All right—all right. Don't rub it in.'

And then we lapsed into silence, while the Buick ate up the miles. Before long we were travelling in the Oxford direction, and the car kept up a steady fifty miles an hour. Cator drove well. Elsa smoked continuously. I was satisfied to be quiet with my thoughts and the knowledge that I was now in a position to do more to defeat the Withered Man than anyone else in England.

If von Horssell had been completely deceived.

14

I am Trapped

It was significant that no attempt was made to blindfold me. That, added to the way in which the 'rescue' had been effected, convinced me that von Horssell was satisfied with my *volte face*, and yet I found it hard to believe. The explanation of that is simple: the German takes it for granted that for money or safety a man will change his colours, and the British work normally on the assumption that, whatever else, a man will be loyal

We reached the main Reading–Basingstoke road in about an hour but it was not long before we were heading west-north-west. Although it was getting dark I watched the garages carefully. One thing startled me—and worried me. The number which had the word 'Star' in the name was surprisingly high: I put it at one in ten. All of them were small places, run by one or two men, but all were also danger spots. Some, of course, must be genuine and loyal.

I wondered how long these preparations had been going on.

I felt again a sense of depression which was not improved by my occasional bitter comments about Holt. And then—a task which proved even more difficult—I commented once or twice on Mary's attitude. I saw Elsa's eyes narrow, and quietly she asked:

'So—the woman Dell is not faithful, Murdoch?'

I said: 'I won't talk about that.'

She said nothing more, but her leg, from knee to thigh, pressed against mine for the rest of the short journey.

We pulled up eventually outside a large house, standing well back from the main road, some three miles outside Oxford. There were painted signs, which read:

The Lumley Nursing Home

Highest Medical and Surgical Attention

Nothing could appear more innocent than that, and I judged that as well as garages, von Horssell had a string of these nursing-homes up and down the country. When I went inside I saw that it was an entirely different place from the one I had left that morning, but as we entered a nurse came out of a room on the left of the hall, closing the door very quietly.

'Upstairs,' Elsa said.

I was shown into a barely furnished bedroom, and was not sorry for a wash. I wished it could be a bath. I had been in the room for fifteen minutes when a servant brought in coffee and biscuits, and I reflected that they intended to make me as comfortable as they could. I was beginning to chafe under the inaction when my head jerked up involuntarily.

Thump. A pause. *Thump—thump—thump.*

My heart beat faster, and there was nothing I could do to stop it.

The door opened, and the ferrule of the ebony stick poked through. I assumed a semblance of nonchalance, but

105

I felt a chill run down my spine as von Horssell entered. His progress was so slow, so laborious, that it seemed a miracle that he could walk at all. It took him sixty seconds to reach a long chair by the window, and he lowered himself into it.

'Vell, Murdoch,' he said. 'So you join us.'

'Yes,' I said sharply.

'Vot made you finally decide?' he demanded, and his queer light-blue eyes were on me.

'Holt—and—my *fiancée*,' I lied.

'So,' said von Horssell, and for the first time I saw something like a smile on his lips. 'Der woman—alvays it iss der woman. It iss goot, Murdoch. Now you are on der side vich vill vin. You are vise. You vill remember the way in vich Holland vos taken—and Norvay and Belgium. So it vill be here. Der day approaches.'

I shrugged.

'The quicker the better. I'm sick of it.'

'Yes,' he said, and repeated: '*Ja*. You can help to make it faster, Murdoch.'

'How?' I demanded.

He eased himself over in his chair, and poked the ebony stick so that the ferrule was against my stomach.

'Understand—this. Holt has der agents, up and down der country. Some I know—others I do not know. You vere one of der men who vould know vere dey are—*ja*?'

'I know the lists,' I said. 'I can't remember them all.'

'*Ach himmel!* Dere vos some vay of telling them?'

'No,' I said, 'there were no signs. Approach to them is always by the counter-sign.'

'Vich is?'

I shrugged.

'I don't know. It is changed every other day. I haven't known one since—Monday morning.'

He shrugged his shoulder in turn.

'It cannot be helped. You vill haff a list of der places

106

ve know. You vill add to them all that you know. More, Murdoch. You know vere *all* der food centres are in England?'

I tightened my lips.

'Some of them, that's all.'

'Der main ones,' he insisted.

'They're pretty much alike,' I said.

'*Ja.*' He nodded, absently for him. 'It iss vot I know already. But again you vill look through der lists, an' to those I have add those you know.'

'Right,' I said.

'So,' said von Horssell. 'You vill do all that tonight, before you rest. Dere iss little time for you to rest, or for any of us. In a few days now . . .'

He stopped, eyeing me narrowly, yet I showed no expression. But I made a comment.

'As near as that?'

'As near as that,' said von Horssell. 'Murdoch, you can start at vonce—at vonce,' he repeated, and then he stood up, a task so obviously painful that I disliked the thought that even he was in such pain. I preceded him to the door, and then stood aside for him to pass. He beckoned me after him. The passage was no more than ten yards long, but it took thirty seconds or more to get along it.

At the end of the passage was a wheel-chair, with a nurse in attendance. von Horsell lowered himself into it, and the woman assisted him expertly. She wheeled the chair to a lift not far away, and I went in with them.

We went upwards.

Von Horssell was taken out on the third floor—as far as I could judge from that quick upwards flight—and again he was wheeled to the door of a room outside which a man stood on guard. Cumbersomely the Withered Man stood up, but as he touched the floor with his withered leg he gasped, and sagged downwards. He would have fallen had I not jumped forward and, with the nurse, supported him.

He swore beneath his breath, and then muttered:

'Der injection—get it.'

The nurse nodded and hurried away. I helped the man into the room, the door of which he unlocked with a key he took from his hip pocket.

Inside, it was a large office.

There were filing cabinets round the walls, and in one corner a large desk. Near that was the inevitable long chair. Von Horssell sat in it until the nurse returned. She raised the leg of his trousers above the knee, and jammed home the hypodermic needle. His lips tightened but he made no other sign. She withdrew the needle, and after a few minutes he stood up with much greater confidence.

For some minutes, in fact, he moved as if there was nothing seriously the matter with him, and during those minutes he worked with feverish energy. He drew out drawer after drawer of the filing cabinets, pulling out files of papers and handing them to me. I saw that his cheeks were flushed and his eyes unnaturally bright. But as the minutes passed his breathing began to get laboured.

Finally he leaned away, and stumped to his chair.

'You vill start,' he said.

I sat at the desk, the only place available, and opened the files. Listed on separate cards were details of dozens —no, hundreds!—of the Pink 'Un's agents in this country.

There was, of course, a way of finding them, but there was no need to tell von Horssell. The Pink 'Un had an unofficial register. To read it, copies of A.A. and R.A.C. handbooks were necessary, for the Pink 'Un used garages as well as von Horssell, and also many hotels. There were other trades directories needed also, for there were agents of S.1 in many shops and unlikely places, a powerful, formidable list of names and addresses running into thousands.

I counted those that von Horssell had, swiftly.

There were a hundred and eleven, and I was relieved

at the knowledge that he had little more than a tenth, serious though that was. I was conscious of von Horssell's eyes on me all the time.

I began to write swiftly on spare sheets of paper. I knew a hundred addresses in addition to those here, and I made sure that I put them down completely, comprehensively. I worked with such intensity that I even forgot just what I was doing, but finally I came to the end of my list.

Suddenly I heard: *Thump!*

I started, and swung round.

He was almost at my side, and yet had managed to get out of his chair swiftly and with hardly a sound. He nodded when he read the list, and I think he was satisfied that I was doing all I could.

'Good,' he said. 'And now der food distribution centres.'

My knowledge was not so comprehensive there, but his was. Of the sixteen hundred such centres in the country, he had nearly forty per cent registered. I added a few, and then I looked across at him.

'Thats all,' I said. I was aware of an overwhelming tiredness.

He nodded.

'It vill do for tonight, Murdoch.'

I followed him out of the room. An armed guard was standing outside the door, and he gave the Nazi salute as we passed him. Neither of us responded. Von Horssell relocked the door, and slipped the keys into his pocket.

As we neared the head of the stairs, he faltered in his step.

I gripped his arm.

'Are you all right?'

Obviously he was not. He was perspiring, and beads of sweat were on his forehead and his upper lip. He was breathing heavily and convulsively—and then abruptly he collapsed.

I stopped him from falling.

In that split second the man was completely in my

power, and it flashed through my mind that although the result would be death for me, I might do an inestimable service to my country if I killed him. It would have caused no compunction to have strangled him with my bare hands, but . . .

Others worked with him, and Holt wanted the *full* plans.

We were out of sight of the guard, and I acted swiftly. I lowered the Withered Man slowly to the floor, and then felt for his case of keys. I recognised the peculiar shape of the one with which he had opened the records office door, and I slipped it from its hook. Then I put the case back in his pocket, and hurried down the stairs. I reached the landing as a nurse came from one of the rooms.

I told her what had happened.

'He works too hard,' she said, and nodded as if this was by no means an unusual development. She went back into her room, and while I waited two men and another nurse arrived. I watched them go up to von Horssell, and would have followed but for the fact that Elsa came hurrying up the stairs below me.

'Stay here,' she said, and then: 'How bad is he?'

'He collapsed completely.'

'He will take a day to recover,' she said, and her lips parted, as viciously as when I had first seen her smile. 'The fool, why did he not rest?'

'Elsa!' I barked. 'It is the Baron von Horssell!'

She drew a sharp breath, and eyed me with an expression which was evidence that she was startled by the sharp rejoinder.

'Yes,' she said. 'Yes.'

And then she laughed, almost as hysterically as I had done earlier in the evening.

'It is late,' she said, at last.

I glanced at my watch and saw that it was nearly half-past one. It was not difficult to understand the weariness

I felt, or the burning at my eyes. I stifled a yawn, and muttered:

'Which is my room?'

'Why not share mine?' she asked.

I barked: 'I don't give a damn where I sleep, as long as I sleep.'

I found it hard to believe, a few minutes later, that I was really alone in the barely furnished bedroom where I had been earlier. The bed was turned down, and there were pyjamas and a dressing-gown. I eyed them longingly, but stepped to the hand-basin, and washed my face in icy cold water. A toothbrush and paste were on the glass plate, and I used them.

I felt much fresher when I had finished.

I changed quickly, and was slipping into a pyjama jacket when the door opened. Elsa appeared for a moment, and she looked ravishingly beautiful. I believe she had been back to her room and made-up.

'You're sure?'

I could only just hear the word.

'I'm quite sure,' I said.

My heart was beating fast, for I was afraid that she intended to stay. It was not a matter of morals: there are few things I would not have done to win through against von Horssell and there are things which Mary would understand—if, indeed, she had to know. But I wanted to leave my room and revisit that office. As I stood watching her, stifling another false yawn, I even played with the idea of attacking her if she did stay, and wondered whether it would be necessary to kill her.

An odd thought, just then.

She shrugged, and blew me a kiss.

'I am in the next room,' she said. 'On the right.'

I nodded, and without waiting for her to go, slipped into bed. I saw her framed against the doorway for a few seconds, and then she went out and closed the door softly behind her.

I lay there for five minutes.

All thought and inclination for sleep had gone. My heart was hammering as it had never hammered before. I imagined time and time again that I heard sounds, but knew that it was purely hallucination. I waited until I was reasonably sure that von Horssell had been taken to his room, and that there was little chance of anyone but the guard being about the house.

I slipped from the bed.

It creaked, and I stood still as I waited for a sign that someone had heard me. No such sign came. I dragged on my socks—there were no slippers—and stepped to the door. It would not have surprised me had it been locked, but it opened without trouble, and I stepped through.

But I had not gone a yard along the passage when I heard a footstep behind me. I swung round, and saw Cator.

15

And I am Busy

I do not think that he had special instructions to watch me.

I believe that Elsa and von Horssell were convinced that I could now be relied on, and in any case they would be confident of their normal precautions to protect them from trouble. Cator had waited and watched, however—his hatred for me making him refuse to believe in my change of front.

I gathered my wits about me quickly.

'What are *you* doing here?' I demanded, keeping my voice low. Elsa's door was close by.

Cator moved his gun a few inches.

'What are *you* doing out of your room?' he sneered. 'You damned idiot, Murdoch, I've been thinking about you. You wouldn't turn against Holt if he tortured you. Get back into the room!'

I drew a deep breath.

'Don't be a fool, Cator. I want the bathroom.'

'*That* won't work,' he sneered, and he jabbed the gun against my ribs. 'Back you go.'

I knew I would have to obey.

I dared not risk being searched, for the key stolen from von Horssell was in my pocket, and once that was found it would be the end for me. I swore at him, still trying to bluff it out, but I would have gone back to my room had Elsa's door not opened.

Her dressing-gown gaped open.

She said sharply: 'What's this, Cator?'

Cator, more surprised than I, turned abruptly, moving the gun away from me. It was then that I acted, for I could see suspicion in Elsa's eyes. She had seen me get into bed, and there would be no effective bluff with her.

I kneed Cator sharply, and at the same time gripped his gun.

I twisted it out of his grasp in a second, and sent him reeling across the passage, so that he banged into Elsa. The two of them lost their balance, and the shindy threatened to waken the household. But I could do nothing about that, I had to work against them both.

I crashed the butt of the gun down on Cator's head, and there was a sickening *crunch* as the bone cracked. He sprawled across Elsa, but I saw her lips opened for a scream.

I struck her across the mouth. The blow stifled her cry, and I levered Cator away from her with my foot and leg. I went down on my knees, the gun threatening the woman, but she would have shouted had I not clapped my hand over her mouth. She bit, but her teeth slid over the palm of my hand.

She kicked at me, but her shoeless feet did no more than bruise themselves against my thigh. I slipped the gun into the pocket of my dressing-gown, and with the hand thus freed gripped her throat. As my pressure tightened I was able to release the hand which was across her mouth.

She was gasping for breath, and I could feel a little pulse beating in her neck. She writhed, but her movements grew more sluggish as I increased the pressure. Her eyes protruded. In those seconds she looked bestial and ugly—but suddenly her eyes closed and her body went flaccid.

I was prepared for a trick, but when I moved her eyelid I knew that she was really unconscious. Her mouth was bruised, and my thumb marks showed plainly in her neck, which was swollen and red. I lifted her into her own room, and then dragged Cator in.

For a moment I stood on the threshold, but there was no sound in the passage, no hint of movement.

I went in, and closed the door behind me.

Bending down, I felt for Cator's pulse. It was not beating, and there was an ugly red ooze from the back of his neck. I viewed that impersonally, dispassionately, vaguely surprised by the force which I had used.

I made sure that he was dead before dragging the body to the wall behind the door. Then I turned to Elsa, picking her up without much effort and carrying her to her own bed. She was surprisingly heavy, and her swollen face was faintly mottled, the perfect skin blotchy and unattractive. She was breathing heavily, and her lips stirred.

I *knew* that I should kill her then.

This was a total war and no mercy was being shown to innocent, harmless women and children. Here was a woman who was far more dangerous than any combatant.

Yes, I should have killed her.

But I could not find it in me to take her life in cold blood.

I knew that, even while I argued with myself, and then I worked swiftly, using the sash of her dressing-gown to tie her arms and ankles. I gagged her with a handkerchief, then bound a silk scarf from the dressing-table round her mouth and nose to make the gagging more effective.

The wardrobe in the room was large, and there was a key in the lock.

I opened the door and carried Elsa Bruenning to the wardrobe, eased her inside in a half-sitting position, then closed and locked the door on her.

I turned to the door leading to the passage.

I opened it slowly, and looked outside.

There was no one in sight, it seemed that nothing had disturbed the others on that landing. I closed Elsa's room behind me, locked the door and slipped the key into my pocket. I returned to my own room, and dressed swiftly. I did not put on a collar and tie, however, and I rolled my trousers up to my knees before slipping on the dressing-gown. With my hair tousled and my legs and feet bare, no one would suspect that I was almost fully dressed.

My shoes I pushed into the big dressing-gown pockets.

My heart was quite steady, and I felt as cool as I had done for a long time. I knew the odds against me, knew even then that I would probably never get away. But I had burned my boats completely, and must go on.

I reached the third floor.

I knew that the guard would be outside that office door, and I approached the passage quietly. I peered round the edge, and saw the man sitting on a straight-backed chair, looking up towards the ceiling with an air of utter boredom. I walked softly towards him, on a thick carpet. I kept the gun trained towards him: his gun was in his lap.

He did not see me until I was within ten feet of him.

Then he started violently.

His hand moved convulsively towards his gun, and for

a second I was afraid that he would use it. One shot would bring everyone running.

'Drop that gun!' I rasped.

His fingers first clutched, then released it. I covered the remaining few feet swiftly and took the gun from his knees. He cowered back, badly frightened—a man who had been taught to give no mercy and who took it for granted that none would be given to him.

'Turn about,' I said.

He obeyed instinctively, and I cracked the butt of the gun on his head with less force than against Cator. He slumped down in his chair. I left him there and slipped the key into the lock of the office door.

It opened.

I half-dragged and half-carried the unconscious guard into the room, and bound him hand and foot with his own belt and braces. Not until then, nor until I had closed and locked the door, did I really get to work.

The files were sometimes behind locked steel cabinets, but locks can be forced with comparative ease if no attempt is made to conceal the fact that they have been broken. I used a knife and a pick-lock, both specially made tools, and I unlocked each drawer in turn until every one in the room was standing out. There were eight four-drawer cabinets.

I took specimen sheets from every file.

They were carefully catalogued and indexed, which was not surprising: the invariable Teutonic thoroughness made its invariable mistake: von Horssell had assumed that the room was inviolate, and worked on that assumption.

There were records of the food depots and Holt's agents, which I had already seen, but that proved only a small proportion of the whole. There were lists of armament factories and petrol depots, of secret factories and store-houses, there were plans of industrial areas, of underground stores, of secret trial ports and bays. It was the most comprehensive survey of the essential war industries of Great Britain, and although on a small scale I doubt whether it was much less thorough than that at the Ministry of Supply.

It was, of course, useless to try to take all the papers: a lorry would have been needed.

There was no telephone in the office, and even if there had been I had no doubt that there was a private exchange in the house, and that no calls could go through unheard. I knew that two things were essential—to destroy those records, and to get a strong force of police at the house quickly.

The records had to go first.

I decided that after I had examined the windows. They were of the faintly yellow bullet- and soundproof glass which I had seen at the Staines house, and there was no hope of getting out *via* them. To escape and summon the police I had to leave this room, and the records must not be left whole.

I dragged file after file out of the drawers, and littered the floor with the papers. In some places piles were knee-high. Next, I turned my attention to the drawers in the desk. Only one was locked: those which were unlocked were either empty or filled with plain stationery. I forced the one locked drawer, and found in it two small loose-leaf books, and a sheaf of papers small enough to go into my breast pocket. I crammed them in, and then stepped to the door.

No one was outside.

The guard remained unconscious, and I dragged him into the passage and along the landing. Then I returned to the office, and stepped to the far corner. I struck a match, and ignited the first layer of papers. They flared swiftly, and the smoke and flame wafted into my face. I went back a few yards, and started the fire at another point—a second, third and fourth. By the time I was by the door a quarter of the room was already blazing furiously, and the heat was unbearable.

I went out, locking the door behind me.

I glanced at my watch and saw that it was nearly half-past two.

From the landing I could hear the muffled roar of the burning papers, while smoke poured from beneath the door and the smell of burning stung my nostrils. I hurried downstairs, still clinging to the dressing-gown.

When I did meet trouble it came without warning, at a moment when I thought I was safe.

I was on the landing of the floor of my own room, and I could see into the hall. On the top stair I heard the *click!* of an opening door, but it was too late to draw back. Into the hall stepped two men, and a nurse.

And from behind me came a man's voice:

'*Stop vere you are!*'

I had my hand in the dressing-gown pocket, about the gun I had taken from Cator. I turned, and saw one of the manservants standing by an open door, holding a Mauser automatic. I did not hesitate, but fired through my pocket.

The man went down.

The muffled roar of the shot followed the pained expression of surprise on his face, and was followed by the thud of his falling body. The trio downstairs were staring upwards, and I saw one of the men move his hand towards his pocket.

I fired, and missed.

A bullet came towards me, and I felt it pluck at my dressing-gown as I rushed down the stairs. My second bullet took effect, and the man went down. The nurse was racing along the passage by the stairs, screaming at the top of her voice. The remaining man darted into the room from which he had come.

Through the screaming and the thud of my own footsteps I heard the key turn in the lock.

I reached the front door while other doors opened, other shots were fired. As I drew back the bolt of the door a bullet smashed through the coloured glass not an inch from my head, and splinters streaked my forehead as instinctively I ducked. I felt a sharp pain at my left eye, and I could not see out of it.

An unnatural coolness filled me, but I *was* cool. In spite of a bullet which plucked against my dressing-gown and another which buried itself in the wood of the door an inch from my hand, I forced the chain and bolts back, and twisted the handle. The door yielded.

I glanced over my shoulder.

There were two men at the head of the stairs, but I knew why they were shooting badly—they looked bleary-eyed and hardly awake.

I banged the door behind me.

Glass shattered from it as I left the porch. I ran on grass which grew along the drive, but my feet were cut by stones from the few yards of gravel. I fired behind me, emptying the first gun, fired again with the one I had taken from the guard.

Shots followed me, but did no damage.

Moreover, the shooting from the house stopped with miraculous speed—miraculous as far as I was concerned, for I was a clear mark for anyone who really took aim. The moon was high, and although it was still young spread a radiance which showed everything in clear, serene relief.

And then I heard the engine of a motor-cycle nearby.

I reached the drive gates as an A.A. scout on night duty for the L.D.V. drew up, and he sprang from the seat with a rifle in his hands.

I gasped: 'Radio—or 'phone—for help. Men here—mustn't get—away!'

He said with commendable coolness: 'The 'phone's half a mile down the road, sir.'

'Give me the rifle,' I snapped. 'Get that—message—off.'

Of course, he should not have given it up so easily, and I was afraid that he would refuse. But my desperate appearance probably convinced him that I was right—that, coupled with a fresh burst of shooting from the house. He let me take the heavy service rifle, and jumped back on his machine. By the time he had started, he was blowing on a piercing instrument which deafened me and sounded high above the roar of the engine.

I threw myself face downwards on the grass by the drive gates, sighting the head of the drive with the rifle. I knew that von Horssell's men would make a desperate effort to get away, and that I could do little to stop them. That was hardly in my mind before the first car started from the rear of the 'nursing-home', spraying machine-gun bullets. I fired three times, but the tyres were protected and the sides of the car were probably bullet-proof.

I had to fling myself behind a stone pillar for safety.

From there I fired again, but the car had reached the road and swung along it with tyres screeching and engine whining. I heard a second from the house, and a third. My shooting was futile; the vicious bark of machine-guns, the deadly *tap-tap-tap* echoing in my ears was incessant.

The second car roared past me, and the third.

There were a few minutes of comparative silence, and then I saw the front door open, and saw two men carrying a stretcher towards a car standing there. I fired quickly, but had hardly time to take aim. I could just see the inert form on the stretcher, knowing that it was von Horssell, realising with a frightening desperation that I must kill him.

I hit one of the stretcher-bearers.

But as the man staggered another took his place, and the stretcher was then out of my sight. The man at the wheel of the car started to open fire with his machine-gun.

I crouched for cover, and bullets sprayed the air over my head.

The car engine hummed.

Then, for the first time, I heard sounds from behind me. I had no time to wonder what it was but I heard shooting—rifle-fire I fancied. It was of no avail. The fourth car, the car carrying the Withered Man, swung round the drive gates, and hurtled along the road. It was a hundred yards ahead of the small military car which came rushing in pursuit.

I saw the military car swing across the road and crash into some trees. It was going at such speed that the crash shook the ground on which I was lying, and a split-second later it burst into flames with a roar and a blast which sent débris smashing into the stone pillar near me.

Débris flew through the air, and I covered my head with my hands, but was unable to avoid the piece of wreckage which crashed into the back of my head. I hardly felt pain. I felt my senses reeling, there was a red sheet in front of my eyes—followed by blackness.

16

I am Convalescent

I do not know how long I was there, with the wreckage of the little car burning fiercely and casting a red glow for miles around, with the crescent moon looking down urbanely, lighting a scene as grim as one could conceive in that quiet part of the Oxford countryside. I learned afterwards that it was no more than five minutes before other help came, men brought from a nearby camp by the urgent summons of that invaluable A.A. man.

I did not know that the house was approached by fifty men, but that no shots came from it, and that when it was searched they found three dead men—Cator, the guard, and one other, probably the stretcher-bearer I had hit— but no others. I was not able to tell them to look in the wardrobe for Elsa Bruenning, whom I should have killed.

I did not know that the flames which had taken a hold of the top of the house kept the invading party from the third floor, and that it was nearly twelve hours before the house was in a safe condition to be searched, but that by then the roof had crashed in, and one wing was nothing but a mass of charred and blackened rubble.

I did not know that I was taken to a hospital in Oxford, and that a porter catalogued me as a 'deado' after one swift look. He was a pessimist, that man, for my chief trouble was concussion, which lasted for some days.

Days—at that period in the war!

Happily, I was unaware of the urgency of it all, for my mind was blank about the immediate past, and only occasional things flitted through my mind concerning it. A pert, snub-nosed nurse who enjoyed flirting chaffed me as soon as I was able to sit up.

'Who is Elsa?' she asked, and I forced a smile: I did not like to think of Elsa, for I could imagine her fast in that wardrobe in the heat of the fire. I hoped she had not regained consciousness.

'An old friend,' I said.

'Old flame, more like,' she retorted, and made me wince. 'You were always shouting her name while you were unconscious, Mr. Morely.'

'Morely' was the name I had given the hospital authorities when I had come round; and Pinky knew the *nom de guerre*.

When I was fit enough to think more or less normally, I was filled with a sharp depression.

There was a sense of complete failure, bad in itself but

made worse by the fact that Pinky did not come to see me. The nurse gave me a little information about the nursing-home, but she varied her story so often that I knew she was calling on her imagination. I knew that von Horssell had escaped, but I could not be sure that he had not been followed.

The papers told me little.

They did not make cheerful reading. It was another of the dark periods for England. There was bombing and attempted landings, there was fierce activity on the Western Front and it seemed as if we were continually on the retreat. Neutrality, in Europe, was confined to Eire and Sweden—and there was a worrying lack of news of activities on the other fronts. No news was not good news, in those days: they would have given us all the good news they could, for the people needed cheering, despite the grim determination with which they waged the war that had been brought home to them with such awful intensity.

No news, no word from Holt, nothing from Ted, or Mick, or Mary. I was lying in a private ward, and the loneliness was at times almost unbearable. At least I was improving quickly. The bandages about my head were removed after three days—I had received only a slight scalp wound, although my knees, arms and elbows were badly bruised.

After the sixth day, I was able to get up.

I felt weak on my pins, but my head was quite clear and I could remember everything that had happened vividly. I had written two reports, in the peculiar shorthand which Holt taught me years before, and was assured by the hospital authorities that they were sent by special messenger to the general office of S.1 in Whitehall.

On the ninth day I was told that I was to be sent to Devon for convalescence.

My treatment could not have been bettered, although my progress might have been retarded when, after I had first walked through the grounds, I saw numbers of wounded soldiers convalescing.

For the first time I dwelt on the possibility of the Allies losing the war. What drove that from my mind was the cheerfulness of men recovering from dreadful wounds, men who declared in grim earnest—they who so often were jocular in face of all adversity—that they would rather die a dozen times than let the Nazis gain an inch of British soil.

They knew what Nazi-ism meant, and so did I.

They had seen the machine-gunned refugees and heard the pitiful cries. They had found themselves faced with almost impossible odds, when Leopold of the Belgians gave his fateful order and perhaps lost a throne, forever. They had suffered the biggest blow of all when the octogenarian Marshal Pétain made his terms, but they had no thought of surrender. They *knew* it would be better to die than to live under Hitler.

I knew, too.

And I think it was the knowledge of the essential right of our cause that kept defeatism at bay. After the first few minutes, I enjoyed my spell with the Tommies. But I was whisked away in secrecy and after dark one night. I had been warned to be dressed and ready for a journey by nine o'clock, and it was nine-fifteen when the snub-nosed nurse came, a little woebegone.

'I'd been hoping you'd stay for a while longer, Mr. Morely, you've cheered us up no end.'

'You've mended me,' I said, patting the starched sleeve of her uniform. 'Keep the gleam in those eyes, colleen, and remember a smile will often do more damage than a bullet.'

She laughed, more light-heartedly.

'Och, and it didn't to you,' she said, and she saw me downstairs to the waiting car.

I did not recognise the chauffeur, and was almost afraid

at one stage in the journey that this was another ruse from the Withered Man. But after half an hour we slowed down, and I knew it was all right. The slotted headlamp masks gave enough light for me to recognise the solid figure standing on the kerb of a village street. The door of the car opened, and in the dim interior light I saw Percy's chunky face, Percy's wide grin. He grabbed my hand and pumped it up and down, and then asked me if I minded him riding in the back with me.

'While you behave yourself, of course,' said I.

'I ain't never goin' not to agine,' said Percy with feeling. The springs creaked as he lowered himself to the seat, and then called to the chauffeur: 'All aboard, old cock, get a move on.'

The same old Percy!

He was silent for a few moments. The light was very dull, and I could only just see his tanned countenance. Sheepishly, he began:

'I ask you, Guv'nor, was it fair? Puttin' it across me like that? You might 'ave given me a wink.'

I steeled myself.

'Percy,' I said, 'you're an ungrateful, mistrusting son of a boiler-maker, and you don't deserve the wages I've been paying you for the past ten years.'

'Oh, Lord!' groaned Percy. 'S'elp me, I didn't mean it, I fought—thought,' corrected Percy, who remembers his pronunciation under stress, 'I fou—thought, I means, that you'd gone crazy, it looked as if you'd been drugged or somefink.'

Sepulchrally, I growled: *'You ruddy swine.'*

'No, come orf it,' said Percy in alarm. 'Don't keep it up. I mean—Guv'nor, I shall begin ter believe you're goin' to take it out of me! You put it over proper, I'll say that for you. Did I say ruddy to *you*?' he went on in tones of disbelief. 'I can't remember, s'elp me I can't.'

'You misbegotten liar.' I laughed from sheer good spirits.

'All right, Percival, I'll forget it. Now tell me everything.'

'She's fit an' well,' said Percy understandingly. 'I 'opes you won't go for 'er the way you've been for *me*,' he added reproachfully. 'She can't stand it, I don't mind tellin' yer. Proper orf colour she's been, but only in 'er spirits, mind you.'

'Where is she?' I demanded.

'Oh, at the pub,' said Percy off-handedly. 'Kind of place you likes. Pinky's booked as Mr. and Mrs., sir.'

'Refer to your commanding officer as Sir Robert,' I said without much feeling. My heart leapt at that information, for Mary and I had often worked as a married couple in the past.

I lapsed into silence, and Percy did not interrupt until I said suddenly:

'Did Sir Robert get my messages, do you know?'

'Yessir—at least I fink—think so,' said Percy.

I could get no more out of him, and we were driven in silence for over an hour. By then the moon was at its height, and once or twice I saw it shimmering on the silvery stretches of the sea. I saw cargo boats making their way up the Severn—I guessed where we were—and ahead of me I could see the winding road, with the cliffs that stretched down to the sea. It was so quiet and peaceful, and the glow from Percy's cigarette had a queer comforting effect.

We passed some tiny cottages on either side and then the road went steeply downwards. The moon shimmered on the rocks on either side of us, on trees in full coverage of leaves, on shrubs and granite crags. Finally we pulled up outside a small inn, which appeared to be cut off from the world except for that steep, winding road. The foreshore was no more than a hundred feet away from the courtyard of the inn.

I heard a door bang.

Percy urged me out of the car first, and footsteps clattered on cobbles as I stood down. A moment later Mary was in my arms, and I felt whole again. I felt her heart beating fast as she pressed against me, and her heavy breathing, excited—and more than excited. I guessed what she was feeling, and I have never loved her so much as I did when she was telling me without words that she had doubted.

I knew that she would suffer more than I for that, and I must help her as much as I could.

.   .   .   .   .

We talked far into the night.

It was warm, and most of the time she was curled up on the coverlet of my bed, her head resting against my shoulder, tendrils of her hair wafting about my cheeks. From time to time she would grip my arm and my hand. She seemed very young then, and very helpless—the Mary who had always been so capable and loyal, the Mary on whom Holt often preferred to rely. She had talked about her anger with herself when finally Pinky had told her the truth. The photographs which von Horsell had sent—there were others than the one, I learned, and she did not know they were faked—had started the doubt in her mind, and Percy's story had increased it. Then Pinky had announced that the evidence was all against me.

'But,' she said fiercely, 'I should have known better, darling. I feel the biggest beast in the world!'

'The place is reserved for Adolf,' I said lightly.

That changed the subject, almost unwittingly.

'The Nazis are doing well in France,' she said.

'How well?'

'Too well,' said Mary, and for the first time she slipped from the bed and stepped to the open window. We had no light but the moon, and her silhouette was breathtakingly lovely. She put her hands up to her hair, and coiled the waves that fell to the back of her neck. 'I'm almost frightened sometimes.'

'What does Pinky think?' I asked.

'I don't know. I haven't seen him for nearly a week. I'm convalescing too.'

'The confounded liar!' I exclaimed.

She laughed.

'You mean Percy? I told him to tell you I was all right. I am, really—there was a little smash when I was driving, and I escaped with bruises and slight concussion. Never mind that now—Bruce, did you tell Pinky all you knew in the notes you sent him?'

'Yes—everything.'

'It's queer. There was no sign of the woman Elsa.'

I stiffened.

'He couldn't have had the right room searched.'

'He did—he told me on the 'phone. The first floor was hardly damaged, and every wardrobe was examined on the morning after the fire. She wasn't there.'

I whistled.

'She couldn't have escaped on her own, that's certain.'

'She escaped, somehow.'

I felt gloomy and depressed again, the magic of Mary's company was dimmed.

'Elsa's loose, then, and von Horssell. Between them they're formidable. I—oh, well, what's the use of worrying while convalescing, sweetheart? I'm tired, and you're tired. Let's get to sleep.'

They were good days that followed.

A note from Pinky reached me on the following morning. He told me that there was plenty to be done, but that things weren't quite ripe yet. He added

You did a lot to spike von H.'s wheels. Good work! The P.M. as well as others are very pleased. Now listen! I've given you Mary and Percy and a car and a spot you like.

128

Do your job properly—get fit. Fit, fit, fit! I'll be wanting you all, soon, and it may be for the final crack-up. R.H.

In the daylight I found that the inn was as lovely a place as one could wish, thatched and yet spotlessly clean, and with a landlord who exuded confidence and good spirits, drank cider and told us how he would win the war each evening—and each morning when we gave him the chance. A short man, colossally round at the middle, he had a thin wraith of a wife who echoed all his words with: '*That's* right, Matty, *that's* right.'

A few customers came from nearby hamlets and fishing cottages, but there were no other residents. The small bay and short stretch of golden sands running down to the sea were ours except for lobster pots and fishermen busy a few hours a day. The swimming was perfect, and that spell of weather grew hotter and more superb. We grew tanned, and even bronzed, we ate plenty and we could not have asked for a better 'honeymoon'.

It ended when we least expected it—about midday on a day so hot that even in bathing costumes it was difficult to get cool. We had taken sandwiches to a sandy cove some distance from the inn, and into the bay came Percy, pulling heavily on the oars of a small dinghy. His voice came travelling over the tranquil seas:

'*The—Boss—is—waitin*'!'

Mary and I began to pack up the picnic case at once. By the time Percy had pulled inshore we were in our dinghy, and I was following Percy back to the bigger bay. Smoke curled lazily from the chimney of the kitchen, and the 'Fisherman's Rest', with its white walls and burnished thatch, a few late ramblers and beds of roses and antirrhinums, appeared a place of sleepy serenity.

The snug lines of Pinky's Daimler destroyed that illusion.

Pinky was waiting in my room. He was sprawled by

the open window, fanning himself with a white-brimmed Panama hat, and his neck bulged over his silver-grey collar. His short stubby legs stuck out in front of him, and he had kicked off his shiny brown shoes, and was wriggling his toes. Thus Sir Robert Holt, O.B.E., Chief of British Intelligence (S.I Branch) and, although I say it myself, the cleverest and shrewdest Intelligence chief in Europe.

His bright blue eyes were wide open.

'Come on, come on,' he said testily, and struggled up to a sitting position. 'Glad to see you, Bruce. Damned fine job you did—haven't forgotten it and not likely to. Everything considered I don't think it could have worked out any better, but I'd like to know just how it developed.'

'Have a drink,' I said, 'and I'll tell you.'

Over cider, I gave the story as concisely as I could. He nodded from time to time, increasing the number of his chins. When it was done, he nodded, drew in a deep breath and then puffed out his cheeks.

'Pheeee-eeew!' he exclaimed. 'Quite a time you had, me boy, quite a time! We lost you at that one-eyed one-star garage place. Had you until then. Next we heard was of the machine-gunning and whatnot, and a description of you.' He didn't wait for me to ask questions. 'Well, now. Your notes told me what you'd destroyed. For a while I was on top of the world, right on top of the world. However, come back to that. I've done a lot since then. I've rounded up the Star garages, although I don't know how many others might be involved. I've had every damned nursing-home in the country raided, and we've closed up eleven—found all the proof we wanted that von H. used them. But—no more records.'

'You wouldn't expect to find a card index and filing system at every place,' I said.

'No,' admitted Pinky. 'Quite right, I wouldn't, but I didn't find anything in the way of information. Each place was fitted out with a transmitting station, but I don't think they'd been used. They were part of the whole organisation, Bruce. I fancy that von H. was—I mean, is—preparing for the major invasion, that it might have started by now but for you, and the fact that I could work fast. But— we didn't beat him, we only postponed his effort.'

'Are you sure?' I demanded sharply.

'Yes,' said Pinky, 'I learned it from you. Those papers you stuffed into your pocket. There was information there that he has *four* places like the Oxford house dotted about the country. Four less one still equals three. See your job now, Bruce? Find the other three.'

17

The Parlour

That evening there were two holidaymakers in the 'Fisherman's Rest'. They were, they said, taking a spell from heavy war work, which was an apology to mine host, who seemed to think that anyone in full health should be thinking of other things than holidays. One was a tall, melancholy-seeming man, and the other short and thickset. Neither of them fished, they said. They just wanted to be lazy. A bit of swimming, perhaps, and sun-bathing. They eyed Mary freely, and had I not known them better I might have been annoyed.

Mick and Ted had arrived.

We did not acknowledge our previous acquaintance, and even avoided contact with them in the hotel by night. They knew what to expect and what to do in emergency. Pinky had brought with him three sub-machine-guns, three automatic rifles, a number of automatic pistols, plentiful ammunition, hand grenades, and another few oddments of lethal weapons.

The idea had been in his mind, of course, before he had come down on his flying visit. For the 'Fisherman's Rest' was an ideal defensive spot. It could be approached only by the one steep road, and high cliffs, most of them falling sheer into the sea, was the only other means of approach by land. The only way men could have been sent from the top of the cliffs to the cove was by ropes, and that would give plenty of time for working in.

Approach from the sea was unlikely, and was guarded against by a machine-gun nest which we built against the cliffs at one side of the inlet. The inlet itself was no more than a hundred yards across, and inside the bay widened until it was almost a land-locked lake. The water, however, was shallow—at no point was it more than ten feet deep, and the yellow sands at the bottom were visible in most weathers.

Of the four men, one slipped out each night after dark, and was at the machine-gun nest until three o'clock, when another relieved him. The road at the top of the cliffs was being guarded by two other agents who had taken possession of a deserted fisherman's cottage.

Three days brought nothing: the fourth day brought a small motor-boat skimming across the surface of the water at the inlet to the cove. I was in my room at the time, changing. Percy was on guard by the machine-gun nest. Mary was somewhere in the grounds with Ted, and I could hear Mick in his room, next to mine.

Hearing the stutter of the motor-boat's engine I looked out of the window. A young man in white flannels and an open-necked shirt lolled in the boat, and a dark-haired girl in shorts and a brassière-topped swimsuit was at the tiller. I would have noticed nothing unusual but for the high speed of the little craft.

It *was* coming fast—so fast that there seemed a possibility that it would pile up on the shore. The girl held her course until the last moment, and then swung the helm round hard.

I shouted: 'Look out, Mary!'

I felt a quick panic amounting to horror, for from the window I could see the young man move, uncovering an automatic rifle and a sub-machine-gun in the boat. He had the machine-gun into position before I swung round to my dressing-table for an automatic. As I pulled, the stutter of the gun was echoing through the clear air, and from the grounds of the 'Fisherman's Rest' I heard a shout —a woman's cry of pain.

I heard the roar of Mick's automatic from the next room, and when I reached the window, gun in hand, I could see the spurts of water close to the boat, which was sweeping round the bay, some ten yards from the edge. The girl still crouched over the tiller, the man was sprawled on his stomach in the bottom of the boat and using the machine-gun. I heard the splatter of bullets against the wall of the house beneath me, and I kept close to the inside wall while I fired. On my second shot a spray of bullets came through the open window, and struck against the far door.

It stopped abruptly.

The man in the boat heaved upwards, and then fell in an awkward angle across his gun. Thus the attacking fire stopped, and the girl swung the boat straight towards the gap and the wide sea. I hurried out of my room and almost banged into Mick Fuller, whose rugged face was anxious, his thickset body moving with speed. But I reached the head of the stairs before him, and halfway down swung myself over the banisters. The floor of the hall creaked as I landed, and I heard a gasp from the tap-room door.

Outlined against it was mine host, mouth agape and paunch aquiver.

'Mis—Mister Morely . . .'

I reached the sun-swept courtyard of the inn. I had one

concern and one only—for Mary. I shouted as I ran towards the beach, but my shout was drowned in another burst of machine-gun fire. This time it was from Percy, mounting guard by the rocks. I saw the bullets sweep into the water just aft of the motor-boat, which was travelling at great speed and with a stuttering roar that mingled with the firing, and turned that haven of peace into Bedlam.

And then I saw Mary. She was on her knees, *unhurt*.

I drew a deep breath of relief and reached her side. Ted Angell's tall figure was by the water's edge, and he was firing with his automatic towards the fast retreating boat. Nothing made Ted hurry.

Mary was kneeling beside the still figure of one of the maids of the 'Fisherman's Rest'. Across the girl's white apron, a little higher than her stomach, was a line of red where the bullets had struck her: they must have torn her almost in two, but had missed the heart and therefore had not brought the merciful instantaneous death.

I stepped roughly in front of Mary.

I need not dwell on what followed.

Nor on the next hour, for police and L.D.V. officials arrived, summoned by a fisherman who had heard the shooting, and rushed to the nearest telephone. Mine host had lost all of his *bonhomie* but there was no reproach in his attitude.

A doctor arrived, although too late, and the girl's body was taken away in an ambulance. I told the local inspector from Lynton enough to make him understand that he could not expect a full explanation. Percy came over in the dinghy which served the machine-gun post, pale-faced and angry with himself.

'I couldn't've missed, Guv'nor,' he greeted me. 'I tore pieces out've that ruddy boat, I know I did.'

'Never mind that, I said with acerbity. 'Get back to the gun, they might try again.'

'Gorblimey,' said Percy, and he made for the dinghy at the double.

By then Mary had telephoned S.1 with a report, but most of the newcomers to the 'Fisherman's Rest' had gone, and there was quiet again. The only tell-tale signs of that swift and ruthless attack were the bullet marks in the walls, smashed glass, and the dark patch on the grass where the maid had died.

I had a word with Dibble, the landlord, and he showed so much understanding that I suspected he had been warned.

'You'll let me know how her people are placed, won't you?' I said. 'They'll get compensation of course. And if it would help if I had a word with them, let me know.'

'Mebbe they'd appreciate it, sir,' said Dibble. 'Known old Tom Langley all've my life, I have. An' Lil.' He shook his fat head slowly, and his usually rosy cheeks were pale. 'I never would have thought Millie would have gone out that way, sir.'

That was all: he asked no questions.

The girl had taken the motor-boat to safety, although there was a chance that it would founder before it was far from the shore. The only motor-boat in the bay, belonging to Dibble and with a powerful engine, had been struck by the first burst of machine-gun fire, and was water-logged. Once the attacking craft had gone out of the inlet it had swung towards the south, and had been safely hidden by the cliffs.

A coastguard's launch from Lynton was searching the cliffs for any sign of wreckage, and there was nothing else that I could do. A tight-lipped party met in my room when the police and others had gone.

We could have gone on talking in circles for the rest of the day, of course, but we did not. In the afternoon, a middle-aged fisherman from a village nearby, and a woman dressed in deep mourning—which was remarkably fast work, adding to the pathetic effect she made—arrived to hear just what had happened. They were the maid's parents, of course. They showed a simple desire to know just how she had died, and there was no reproach in their manner. I talked to them for twenty minutes, and they thanked me as if I had been responsible for saving their daughter, not for her death.

Towards nightfall, there came a telegram from London. The local post office sent a boy down the cliff road with it. He reached my room, apparently having received strict instructions to place the buff envelope in my hands and mine alone. He was a gawky lad, with ears that stuck at right-angles from a freckled, mahogany-hued face.

I ripped open the envelope, and read:

Sending Denyer down to you. H.

I stared unseeing at the boy.

'Denyer—Denyer? Oh, of course. No answer, thanks.'

And as he shuffled out I frowned, wondering why Pinky had decided to send young Denyer from the refugee-receiving station to that little inlet on the Devon coast.

18
Young Denyer

Denyer arrived just after ten o'clock.

He came alone, by car. He wore the baggy flannels and the shapeless sports jacket in which I had first seen him, and brought with him vivid recollections of the knife sticking from the back of Father André. Although the evening was cool he had a bead of perspiration on the down of his upper lip.

'By Jingo!' he said as he entered the hall, after pushing past the involved blackout arrangements which Dibble had erected, 'what a journey! I had to stop a dozen times in the last two miles to find the way. And am I hungry!'

Dibble, hovering in the background, announced that supper for the gentleman was served. It was cold ham and salad, and Denyer set to with a will.

'Can anyone overhear us?' he asked, as he ate.

'No,' I assured him. 'This room's all right.'

Percy had instructions to make sure that no one listened at the door. Mick was outside the window, with Mary. Ted was watching by the inlet.

'Good!' said Denyer, with the enthusiasm of a boy. 'I say, Mr. Morely . . .' Pinky had stuck to that name. 'I had the weirdest experience yesterday.'

'Did you?' I said.

'Yes.' He pushed his plate away, and went on tensely: 'I just can't believe it, but it happened. You remember the *curé*? Father . . .'

'André,' I said. 'I'm not likely to forget him.'

'He was buried three days after he was killed,' said Denyer, and then with an unstudied effect which jolted right through me: 'I *saw* him yesterday.'

'*What?*' I cried.

'Sir Robert, or whatever his name is, said the same thing, only stronger. It's a fact though. I knew him so well that I'd recognise him anywhere, and he's been in and out of my mind a lot since that day I met you.'

'You've got his image on your mind so much that you can't get rid of it,' I suggested.

Denyer shook his head vehemently.

'No, it's not that! Sir Thingummy suggested the same thing, but I had something that really made him admit that I wasn't talking out of my hat. Look!' said Denyer, and with a dramatic gesture he took a small photograph from his pocket.

It was the *curé*.

As I looked at it, I reasoned that Pinky would not have sent Denyer here unless he thought there was something in this. I could only think that Father André had a double. I usually suspect the existence of 'doubles', but have come across them too often to scoff without reason.

'When did you take this?' I asked.

'I was near Southampton yesterday,' said Denyer. 'There was a party of refugees going to a village nearby, and I had to look after the billeting arrangements. I saw him'— he touched the photograph—'walking towards me. The moment he saw me he looked away—he's in civilian clothes, you see, and not in his habit—but I managed to get this snap.'

'How?' I asked.

'Before the war I was a dab at amateur photography,' Denyer explained. 'I like to take snaps when people don't realise it. So I bought one of these things. Dreadfully expensive, but it's the only hobby I've got—I don't smoke or drink or gamble,' added Denyer virtuously.

'One of these things' was a miniature camera of the type that can be fitted inside a waistcoat and show little or no bulge. The snapshot is taken by pressing a small bulb, also out of sight, and the highly developed lens and high-speed mechanism ensure a first-class picture. I had seen —and used—similar cameras before.

'Of course,' said Denyer, 'when I started this job I told the authorities about this hobby, and I co-operated with them. That's how I happened to have a photograph of the woman Bruenning. Whenever a bunch of refugees have been suspect,' went on Denyer, 'I've taken a snap without them knowing, and passed it on to the military authorities. That's how I was able to definitely identify several of the men in the billets.'

I began to feel that I had seriously underestimated this young man, but there was the impossible situation that he insisted on maintaining that he had seen Father André, the murdered priest, walking down a Southampton street on the previous day!

'Well, I don't know what to make of it,' I said, puzzled. 'The man was actually buried, you say?'

'Oh, yes.'

'Then it's nonsense.'

'Sir Thingummy said that,' said Denyer, and I hid a smile, for he talked of the Pink 'Un much as the Pink 'Un talked of him. 'Of course, you would think so. But—there are drugs which can induce a state of coma that can pass for death.'

I eased my collar.

Denyer must have talked in this strain to Pinky, and Pinky wanted me to sift the information, the guesswork and the half-formed theories. There might be something else behind Pinky's unexpected messenger.

'Oh yes,' I agreed. 'Drugs which can induce a state of coma that can pass for death. Yes. Ordinary morphia will do it, and . . .'

'Scientists know more about it than we do, of course,' he said. 'But you do admit that it exists?'

'Also,' I said drily, 'I will admit that a five-inch knife stuck in Father André's back, and according to a medical report afterwards received, pierced his heart.'

'Well, I'm only telling what I saw,' Denyer said, no longer smiling. 'Why on earth was I sent down here if you were to be as sceptical as Sir Robert?'

'Let me get this quite straight,' said I. 'You're quite sure that you saw Father André, in full health, walking along a street in Southampton nearly three weeks after he had been buried?'

'That's it,' he insisted. 'I'll swear to it anywhere *and* back my opinion with that photograph.'

'Right,' I said briskly. 'We'll work on the assumption that he's alive. Did you follow him?'

'I tried to, but he got into a car and went off. I was on a bike, and didn't have a chance of keeping him in sight.'

'Then what did you do?'

'Telephoned the Sloane number that I've used before, and Sir Thingummy told me to report to his office straight away. I was up there last night: that's why I'm here. I don't mind what I do, Mr. Morely, provided I can have a stab at these Nazi swine. The more I see of the refugees the more I hate Hitler's guts!' This was strong language from this young gentleman. 'I'm prepared to take any risk, and although my heart condition's a bit tricky, it'll see me through. Er—I'm not likely to live many years, anyhow,' he added.

I stared, and mumbled: 'Well, I'm sorry about that, Denyer. I . . .'

'Oh, you don't have to be sorry,' he said. 'I told you that because it will make you understand more easily that I don't care what happens to me. They won't have me in any of the fighting forces, not even on Home Defence Units. But if you want anyone for a suicide squad, I'm your man.'

He spoke without bravado, which made his offer the more impressive. His gaze did not leave me, and it flashed through my mind that he was half-expecting to be sent out on some forlorn hope then and there. I was now fully aware of Pinky's reason for sending him to me, and I said:

'You told Sir Robert that?'

'Of course I did.'

'Right!' I said briskly. 'We've a lot of room for heroes.' He flushed pink and I went on quickly: 'For the time being, you can do with some rest.'

'I wouldn't say no to a comfortable bed,' he admitted.

Dibble had prepared a room, and I saw Denyer up to it. Then I carried the report to Mary and Mick. They made little comment, and by eleven o'clock we were all in bed, and—I thought—set for a good night.

. . . . .

The first *crump!* came about midnight.

Let there be no mistake about it. Had I been asked I would have said that the little sandy cove with the 'Fisherman's Rest' was absolutely safe from aerial attack. But I was awakened by a terrific detonation which shook the pictures on the walls and crashed the glass from its frames. I was alert in a moment: Mary, in the next bed, was sitting bolt upright.

'Under the bed!' I snapped.

Now that I was awake I could hear the powerful drone of the bomber's engine. It was probably a Dornier, and was flying low. I fell flat on the floor, with Mary on the other side of the room, and the second crash came.

It deafened us, and sent what little glass was left in the windows flying out. I heard a loud rumbling from somewhere nearby, and then a third *crump!* that set the walls shaking; it crashed through the outhouses at the rear of the inn. I could hear someone screaming above the noise of the engine, but by then I was on my feet—that bomber was now heading out to sea. As I passed the dressing-table I grabbed my steel helmet, and jammed it over my head.

Mary shouted: 'A coat, Bruce!'

She was also used to judging the danger, and was now at the wardrobe. She flung a coat towards me while I pushed my feet into my slippers and rushed out. Mick was coming from his room, carrying two service rifles. I grabbed one.

We passed Dibble and two others on the stairs. I remember being surprised that there was no sign of Denyer, and it even passed through my mind that the explosion might have affected his weak heart.

Outside, the night air struck cool.

All of it happened very swiftly, of course, and by the time we reached the beach the droning of the bomber was very nearly out of earshot, and there was a temporary respite.

But it was turning.

I looked towards the inlet. I could see the stars against the dark sky clearly in the gap between the rocks. The reflection shimmered on the sea, which was lapping softly against the sandy foreshore. But the thing that appalled me most was the beam of light that shot towards the skies from somewhere on the cliff edge, perhaps half a mile away.

I snapped: 'See that, Mick?'

Mick's language was more violent than I have ever heard from him as he watched the bomber winging its way back. Another onslaught was coming, but this time the pilot was going to have a shock.

Obviously he could see his target clearly. That damned light gave him his direction, and once he was within range he could see the white-walled building. The dark spread of the wings and body against the sky were like a menacing shadow—as in fact it was, for there was a fast-moving blotch on the surface of the water.

And then from the machine-gun nest by the inlet Ted opened fire.

The sudden stutter of his gun, the flashes of flame and the streaks of the tracer bullets hurtling towards their mark made the moment vivid. Mick and I saw a burst strike the pilot's glass-surrounded cockpit clearly.

Then we fired in turn.

The rifles were not much use against the sides of the plane, but we might get a burst through the hole which Ted had torn. Ted had altered direction, and was following the 'plane, the tracers looking like swift-moving fireflies against the darkness. The barking of our own guns followed, and then:

Crunch!

We flung ourselves face downwards.

I felt the sand bite at my face, and get into my nose and mouth. Then the wind from the explosion lifted a mighty fountain of water over us both, drenching us to the skin.

The next bomb exploded inland.

Mick straightened up, getting the sand out of his eyes.

'Will he try again?' he muttered.

'Depends what he's carrying,' I said.

We knew a moment later that the pilot was not seriously hurt, for the thunder of his engine came again, and he flew low. We kept firing until the last minute, and then flung ourselves down. Ted's gun was stuttering all the time.

There came another roar, different from any we had heard before. A split second later a flash of flame burst from the bomber, and we saw the trail of fire and smoke coming from one of its engines. The machine wobbled.

There was a yellowish red glow for miles about us, and it showed the savage crags and the rocks, reflected on the calm surface of the sea, showed the 'Fisherman's Rest' vividly—even to the smashed ruins of the outhouses.

The bomber was losing height.

'It'll hit the cliff,' I muttered.

The words were hardly out of my mouth before the gap between the bomber and the cliff narrowed, and the final smash came. The flame billowed outwards and upwards, far more terrifying than the fire from the engine. We saw the dark mass of the machine break asunder and then we heard the thunder as the part of the cliff which it had struck began to fall.

The crash was nearly a mile away from us, but in the light of the fiery débris from the bomber we could see the cliff slowly toppling downwards, and almost at once an avalanche of rock and dirt thundered into the sea.

The stars were blotted out.

Mary, bless her, had left nothing to chance. When we got back to the inn we found that she had taken Dibble and the servants into a cellar, and was coming from it when we entered the passage.

'It's all over,' I said. 'Ted got the pilot.'

All Mary said was: 'And you're all right?'

'Except that I've swallowed half of Devon's sand,' growled Mick.

'Do you know,' said Mary sweetly, 'that life without your grousing, Michael, would be the sweetest thing I know. Why don't you go and put it back? Is Ted all right?'

'I'm going to see,' I said.

'What about Denyer?' asked Mick.

'He's still in his room,' said Mary. 'I looked in, and he was under the bed.'

'There are no flies on Mr. Denyer.' I hesitated, and then hurried up to my window, which overlooked the bay. Percy was coming out, and he was beaming with relief.

'I fought you was a gonner that time, Guv'nor.'

'Your luck's still out,' I said. 'Put some clothes on, Percy, we've a climb to make.' I stepped to the shattered window, and shone a torch towards Ted and the machine-gun post. A steady beam came back towards me for ten seconds, which was a signal that he was all right. I shut my torch off, and began to dress.

In five minutes Mick, Percy and I were ready.

Whether there had ever been any chance of finding the man who flashed that message I don't know, but the chance certainly disappeared when we reached the top of the cliff road, for we met a large party of L.D.V. and police. That was reassuring in one way, proving that they were alert and prepared. But by the time I had finished explanations, and dealt with the suspicions of a police inspector who, it seemed, was already worrying about the machine-gunning that afternoon, any chance of finding the spy disappeared.

Nevertheless, I persuaded the L.D.V. to make a search of the South Cliff and, with another bunch of them, went to explore the damage to the North Cliff, where the bomber had crashed.

The body of the pilot was washed up early the next morning, within sight of the inn. He must have been dead before the machine crashed, for there were three bullets in his chest. I had no grief for the man—but wished him alive, for I would have liked some information.

When I was told that the body had been recovered it was nearly eight o'clock. I had managed to get three hours' sleep, but I felt heavy-eyed and my head was aching. One of the first things I did was to go and see Denyer. He had come down soon after I had started out with the search party, and although he was doing his best, he could not hide the fact that he was jittery.

'Well,' I said roughly, 'you've an idea what you're up against, Denyer. Do you still feel like the suicide squad?'

'I—I'll do anything you want,' said Denyer.

And there, for the time being, I left it.

19

Four 'Fatalities'

At half-past nine, the Inspector from Lynton arrived.

A very puzzled and bewildered man, that Inspector Entwhistle. He was short and swarthy, more Cornish than Devon I thought, and by nature suspicious. Whatever suspicions he had harboured of me, however, were gone completely. He asked to see me alone, and when he was in my room he stid:

'Mr. Morely, what do you know of my special orders?'

'Nothing,' I said truthfully.

'Now, come,' said Entwhistle, 'that won't do.' Something like a smile curved his dour lips. 'Oh, well, you know what you're doing, sir. Did you know you were dead, now?'

I stared.

'Am I?'

He cocked an eyebrow.

'I can't believe you don't,' he said, and he handed me a short typewritten memo from the Chief Constable. It read:

Instruct all reporters and others that there were four fatalities in last night's raid. All holidaymakers at the Fisherman's Rest. Messrs. Morely, Angell and Fuller, and Mrs. Morely. Continue to keep all reporters and sightseers from the inn.

'Oh,' I said weakly.

'I had a 'phone call just before I left,' he said, 'telling me to let you see this. The Chief Constable said that you would understand.'

The first glimmer of understanding came then, but it was not until midday that I had it confirmed. By then the telephone wire to the 'Fisherman's Rest' was repaired but, in view of the note, Mary, Ted, Mick and myself had kept out of sight. We could see crowds of sightseers up on the cliffs, but none but accredited agents of the police were allowed to come down. Nor was Dibble—or for that matter his staff—allowed to go up. Soon afterwards a call from the Pink 'Un came.

'Bruce!' he shouted. 'Damn you, why did you let them damage the wires?' He chuckled. 'All right, all right, don't lose your temper. Listen! I've told the Press that you're dead, like Mary and the others. Percy's still alive,' added the Pink 'Un with yet another chuckle. 'I sent word to you through the Chief Constable—did you gather the drift?'

'More or less,' I said. 'Pinky, what . . .'

'Don't call me Pinky!' yelled the Pink 'Un fiercely.

I knew then that he was in high fettle.

'All right,' I said resignedly. 'I'll accept the fact that you think it's necessary for me to be dead, and all that kind of thing. But did you have to send that addle-pated boy scout down to me?'

Pinky roared: '*What!* Do you mean to say . . .'

'I don't exactly disbelieve him,' I said, answering shout for shout, 'but it's a tall story.'

'Hmm,' said Pinky, suspiciously mild in a moment. 'Hmm. You know *why* I sent him down, don't you?'

'Oh, yes,' I said.

'That's good, that's good,' said Pinky with great satisfaction. 'I will say one thing for you, Bruce, I don't have to talk in words of three letters to you. Well, stay there until I tell you to move. It'll probably be this evening, and I'll arrange for you to be taken off from the sea. All right?'

'Right,' I said.

'And follow my instructions to the letter,' went on Pinky. 'To—the—letter, understand. You'll have them by special messenger later in the day.'

'Right,' I repeated.

'Bruce, d'you know I think there's a good chance that we've got von Horssell? Definitely a good chance. Thing is —you know more than you realise, or they wouldn't be quite so anxious to get rid of you.'

'Yes, I'd gathered that too.'

'Don't gather too much,' said Pinky.

He rang off without saying goodbye, and I contemplated the toes of my shoes for some time. When I went out, the door of Denyer's room was standing open, and he was brushing his hair with great care. Not being a young man who paid much attention to his appearance, I wondered why. I did not wonder for long, however, for he hardly moved from Mary during the rest of the trying day.

She reacted—of course—perfectly.

I knew that she was curious as Mick and Ted—and Percy—about our supposed demise, but I could only guess what was behind it, and Pinky would have told me had he wanted me to share my opinion with the others. I pretended, therefore, to be completely ignorant.

Denyer showed a naive interest.

'It's a pretty cunning move,' he acknowledged earnestly, as we had tea in the small lounge. The sun was no longer shining, but it was sultry and too hot, despite the open window and the slight breeze coming through.

'Oh, very cunning,' said Mick, who had less patience with Denyer than any of us. 'I should say that it will easily deceive Hitler. He'll be rubbing his hands all right now.'

'Do you really think so?' demanded Denyer. 'I—oh, damn it!' He broke off. 'There's no need to be funny about it.'

Dibble came in then, and made a beeline for me.

'There's a man with a letter who says he wants to give it to you *alone*, sir.' Dibble had a husky way of talking when serious.

'Where is he?' I asked.

'In the parlour, sir.'

The parlour, a small room with a piano, was a little-used and gloomy room. I did not immediately recognise the youngster who jumped up from a chair with alacrity.

He was a young pilot officer who had joined Holt's brigade some eighteen months before in the chase of von Romain, envoy extraordinary of Berlin.* I had not worked with him since that time but I knew he was still on the Pink 'Un's register. Keen-eyed, fresh-faced, he was shorter than Denyer and about three times as much a man of the world.

He took a sealed envelope from his pocket.

'With Pinky's compliments,' he grinned.

* *Dangerous Journey*, by Norman Deane.

'I'll Pinky you,' I growled. 'All right, go and have some tea with the others.'

'Thanks,' said Graham. 'I'm detailed to stay with you until further orders, by the way.'

I nodded absently, too much concerned with the sealed orders to worry too much about Graham or anyone else. I took the papers up to my room, cut the envelope, and found two foolscap, typewritten sheets. I knew from the many crossings-out and alterations that Pinky had laboriously typed these himself.

His instructions were terse: most of the letter concerned ways and means and possibilities, some of which I already knew or guessed. The essential of the text was:

All of you—including Denyer and Graham—will leave the bay in a small motor-boat which will take you out to sea tonight—starting at ten o'clock. There will be one man in the boat who can be trusted. You will be transhipped at sea and flown to Guildford, Surrey. A car will meet you at the airfield and take you to Dent House, between Guildford and Godalming. After that, use your own judgment.

Read these instructions to all the others.

I scanned the other text again before joining the crowd in the lounge. Denyer was standing by the window, flushed and angry. Mick turned a cherubic face towards me, but I scowled at him.

The atmosphere undoubtedly was unpleasant.

'I don't know what you people are fooling about at,' I said testily, 'but it's time you understood that we've a job on hand and no time for personal quarrels. Hear that, Mick?'

'Yessir,' grinned Mick.

'And now listen to this . . .'

Pinky's orders cheered them, and Denyer lost his anger

149

and started to discuss with Mick the possibility of the Withered Man being at Dent House. Mick was so mild with his sarcasm that no further trouble developed. We had an early dinner, and after it most of us rested; none knew what would be our next chance for sleep.

I think the only one of us who did not sleep was Denyer, who had managed to get more rest than the others. He banged on my door soon after nine o'clock, and opened it without waiting for my call. Seeing Mary curled up on the bed he started back.

'Oh, sorry,' he mumbled. 'I'd forgotten—er—I say, Mr. Morely, I can't make the servants hear.'

'What time is it?' I demanded.

'About ten past nine I suppose.'

I sat up rubbing my eyes.

'They're probably as tired as we are,' I said. 'What do you want?'

'I was hoping they'd make us some tea before we went.'

'If we ask them very nicely,' I said, 'maybe they will.'

I could sympathise with Mick. Denyer was getting on my nerves, but I had more reason for exercising constraint than my friend.

Denyer turned away from the door.

'I'll go and see if I can wake 'em,' he said.

But he did not go far.

I heard a sound outside: an unbelievable sound. I felt a sudden rising of panic, so physical that it threatened to suffocate me. My breathing stopped and my stomach heaved as I heard:

Thump! A pause. *Thump—thump—thump!*

The Withered Man was here!

     .   .   .   .   .

The paralysis which gripped me when I first heard the sound did not last. I was quite sure the man was outside in the passage, and moved swiftly to the dressing-table. An automatic was lying on it. I picked it up, while looking at Mary. I saw her sitting upright in bed, with her clothes on except for her shoes, and she was staring tensely towards the door.

Thump—thump—thump!

Denyer gasped: 'What's that? What's the matter? I— *oooohh!*'

He had turned towards the passage, and I saw him take a step along it. I called out in warning but he either ignored me or was too late. I did not see what hit him, but his body pitched across the threshold of the room.

Before I reached Denyer, however, I saw von Horssell. The first glimpse I had was of his ebony stick, and then the gross figure of the man hove into sight. He was moving with the laborious effort that I knew so well, and his face was quite expressionless in the full light of the bedroom lamp. There was no wind, for the blackout was drawn and the windows closed. The room was hot and stuffy, and that did not help us.

I had the man covered, yet could not rid myself of fear, although the first panic had gone. I looked past him, expecting to see others, but there appeared to be no one else.

He said: 'Put der gun down, Murdoch.'

'I don't trust you as much as that, von Horssell,' I said.

'You haff to,' said the Withered Man, and certainly there was nothing about him to suggest that he was within six feet of a gun. He continued to move, poking the stick towards my stomach and managing to shuffle along with a little pivotal help from his withered leg.

'Keep there!' I snapped.

'*Ach himmel!*' rasped the Withered Man, 'you think I am der vool, Murdoch. Your gun, it iss empty.'

'We'll see,' I said.

But he did not flinch when I turned the gun towards his sound left arm and squeezed the trigger. There was a *click!* but no other sound. I felt a sickening sense of disappointment. I had loaded the gun before going to sleep: someone had been in and had emptied it. Mary's automatic would be empty, too.

'And don't imagine you can use force,' von Horssell said.

Then Mary screamed!

She is not giving to screaming. I think the cry coming from her scared me more than von Horssell himself, and I turned my head. But she was staring at me—towards my stomach. I glanced down, and then I saw why. For there was no iron ferrule at the end of the ebony stick: there was a dagger which glinted cruelly beneath the light, and was not an inch from me.

My mouth was dry.

'You see,' said von Horssell, 'I leaf nothing to chance, Murdoch. I vill tell you more things. *All* der servants here are locked in der cellar, with Angell, Fuller and Briggs. Ve are quite alone but for der fräulein.'

I said, more coolly: 'As thorough as ever, Baron. I congratulate you.'

He ignored the sarcasm.

'But this is not your first mistake,' I went on.

He waved his hand, and the knife at the end of the stick made a circular movement. Had the point been in my flesh it would have neatly disembowelled me.

'A mistake I made, yess, in trusting Cator too much. He vos more in'rested in der personal than der national matters, Murdoch, an' so he giff you der chance that you took. For that I could admire you, but'—his left shoulder shrugged—'you have too much to pay for. Der fräulein as vell as me agrees to that. You attempted to make it seem that you vere dead, Murdoch, but der effort, it failed completely.'

'So it appears,' I said. 'How did you arrive?'

He showed his teeth in what he might have meant for a smile.

'By car, my friend, by car! Vit' me I haff der papers that give me a pass through der cordon. Oh, you haff no need to fear for me, Murdoch. I look after all der things.'

'Yes,' I said. 'You tried to look after me last night.'

He shrugged his one sound shoulder.

'Everything cannot succeed, and now I haff you. There are no chances I take dis time. You an' der woman'—he glanced across at Mary—'vill join der others in der cellar. Den der house, it vill be blown up—from *beneath* der cellar—ven I vant it.'

'An attractive proposition,' I said.

He glanced at Mary again, and his gaze dwelt on her longer than before. Then:

'Ach, you are talkin' for der sake of vords. Fräulein!'

Elsa came in.

It was two weeks since I had seen her, and she had fully recovered from her ordeal. Her skin had its superb lustre, and it was hard to believe that when I had last seen her she had been mottled and patchy, and close to death.

I wished I had killed her.

I did not try to analyse my thoughts, and knew only a sense of utter frustration. Von Horssell had over-tricked the Pink 'Un, and had moved too fast.

Elsa carried an automatic, and she stepped to the dressing-table and sat astraddle on the stool. I knew from that that von Horssell proposed to talk, and I wondered what time there would be at my disposal. But it seemed absurd to think of rescue.

'Is all this necessary?' I said.

'*Ja* it iss!' snarled von Horssell. I have never seen fury so naked in a man's face. His sound leg and arm were quivering. His lips turned back from his teeth and his eyes were glittering and somehow obscene. He rasped: 'You, Murdoch, you alone destroyed der garages I had arranged vit' such care. You destroyed one house of records, you arrange for der raiding of der nursing-home. Because of you I vos reprimanded by der Führer! Der invasion of England vos to haff started ten days ago—because of you I vos compelled to rely on my second means of attack—and to make der arrangements took more time. But—der hour comes! You vill be here. From der radio you vill hear how der invasion succeeds. You vill know of der panic and der vay the country is smashed by der forces of der Fatherland. You vill be in der cellar, vit' your friends. You vill be helpless, although you vill vant to do so much. For der invasion, Murdoch—it comes *tomorrow*!'

20

Von Horssell

There are limits to one's capacity for shock or hurt. I had been completely dumbfounded by von Horssell's arrival, and for some minutes sent right off my balance. Soon, however, my senses had to some degree become numbed. The 'tomorrow', even the vicious way he shouted the word, meant little.

I just did not believe it.

It was something in the nature of an 'it-can't-happen-here' attitude, quite unjustified but nevertheless strong. On his own admission the 'first' line of attack in England had been smashed, and he was asking me to believe that in ten days he had contrived to organise another. No, I did not believe it.

'Don't,' I said distinctly, 'be a bloody fool. You are in the parlour, and the spider is not far away.'

Apparently he didn't follow the inference, but I saw Elsa's lips tighten.

'Talk in vords I know,' he said.

'Right,' said I, and incredible though it may seem I was enjoying myself. 'Sir Robert Holt and I sat down after I had recovered and worked out what appeared to be a foolproof scheme to get you exactly where we wanted. It's worked.'

He stared, quite expressionless.

'You lie, Murdoch.'

'Oh, no,' I said. 'One risk had to be taken. I took it. If I die with you'—I shrugged—'I shall have died in a good cause.'

He turned his head slowly towards Mary.

'And her?'

'We work together,' Mary said.

I blessed her for the calm with which she supported me. I heard Elsa exclaim, softly, and the woman stood up and approached von Horssell. There was a swagger in her walk, and in the woollen knitted dress she looked almost fat: but she remained a beautiful woman: magnificent.

I did not know who else was outside, and whether to believe von Horssell's statement that he was alone but for Elsa. I expected he would have a bodyguard, at least a chauffeur. But if I was uncertain, so were they. I had never seen Elsa so close to alarm.

'A pity, isn't it?' I said conversationally. 'The great invasion due to start, but the Fifth Column commander unable to give the orders for the advance. The Führer'—I turned the word into a sneer—'would be very angry—if you were to live long enough to see him again.'

His tongue darted out and ran along his lips.

'How do you know I am to giff der order?'

'I wonder,' I taunted. 'How do I know your second line of defence, how was I to learn when you planned to start? The defence preparations are all ready, they will go into action the moment the word is given. We *know* where you propose to land troops. We *know* where your stores of arms are in this country. We *know* what districts to expect the parachutroops. We *know* how many tank-carrying 'planes you have. But there isn't,' I added casually, 'the slightest need for me to make a catalogue of them.'

'It iss talk, Murdoch!'

'Really? How many *more* holidaymakers are there in the south? Which is the least likely spot for a landing? This coast, of course. Why do you think we were sent down here? Why do you suppose you were even allowed to bomb us?' I was talking for the sake of talking because I needed time, and yet I was making as much sense as I could. Von Horssell would have given nothing away but Elsa did, and I knew then *why* there had been such desperate efforts to get us killed. Von Horssell *was* to be on the scene of operations, would give the orders to the invaders somewhere on this remote part of Devon.

And Elsa's eyes glittered as she heard me. She snapped:

'He knows. He found those papers!'

She raised her gun.

It happened very quickly, and undoubtedly I would have been dead but for one swift movement from Mary. Mary, unwatched for some minutes, had taken a pillow from behind her, and as Elsa Bruenning moved she hurled it. It struck the woman's hand aside as the bullet cracked, but even then it went close to my head.

I struck at von Horssell, although the sword stick was moving and I felt it tear through the sleeve of my coat. I felt the sharp prick of cold steel, but before it was rammed home the Withered Man had lost his balance, and crashed to the floor.

I was within a yard of Elsa.

I struck at her gun arm and knocked her hand aside; a bullet buried itself in the floor at my feet. She lost her grip on the gun, and it clattered against the wall. Mary moved in a flash and had the automatic before Elsa could reach it. She swung round, and the gun forced the German woman back.

All four of us were breathing heavily.

Von Horssell was stretched out on the floor, quite helpless. I kicked his sword stick out of his reach, then I leaned back against the dressing-table. I heard Elsa say in a strangled voice which held all the fury of the world:

'You fool, Murdoch. This won't save you!'

I stepped to the telephone.

I lifted it, and called the Lynton police. Entwhistle himself answered. I spoke slowly and just loud enough for Elsa and von Horssell to hear.

'Have the cordon of men moved in, Inspector. They'll need the guns, as arranged, but may not have to use them. I've the Withered Man here.'

'*What?*' cried Entwhistle.

'When you've given those orders,' I said, 'ask your Chief to get in touch with London. He will know where to telephone. Have him report that the woman and von H. are prisoners at "Fisherman's Rest". Tell him that all arrangements are working smoothly, and that there is no chance of their escaping. But get that cordon moved in quickly.'

Entwhistle did a praiseworthy best to comprehend.

'You mean you want the place raided?'

'Of course I do,' I said, 'and quickly.'

He rang off with a prompt: 'Right, I'll see to it.'

I replaced the receiver and turned to Elsa. Von Horssell seemed to be right out of the reckoning. I said easily, but with doubt in my mind:

'And so, Fräulein . . .'

Then she tossed the phial.

I had not seen her take it from her blouse and I don't think Mary thought that she was doing more than adjusting her coat. I saw the glint of glass as she threw it towards us, but I was too late to act. The *hiss!* that came as the glass tinkled and broke brought with it a sharp acrid smell, and a fine white vapour. The effect was instantaneous.

I felt as if my head was coming off.

The fumes got into my nostrils and the back of my throat, and seemed to force my head upwards, so that the strain on my neck was unbearable, and I could not breathe. There was a tightness at my chest and burning pain in my throat.

I lost consciousness then.

I had seen nothing from the moment that Elsa had tossed the phial, and did not know that she had fitted a small mask to her mouth and nose before going to von Horssell and putting one on him.

Denyer told me later what happened.

He said also that as soon as Mary and I had collapsed a man in chauffeur's uniform came running up the stairs, a grotesque figure in a service mask. Denyer was conscious, but out of the range of the gas. He told me that he had tried to move, but the blow he had received when the Withered Man arrived had paralysed him.

He watched the chauffeur and the woman hoist von Horssell to his feet. The Withered Man was moved cumbersomely to the end of the passage, helped by the others. Denyer had expected them to shoot Mary and me: apparently the only reason they did not was the arrival of a motor-cyclist on local patrol, instructed by Entwhistle to visit the inn regularly.

There was some shooting.

The motor-cyclist, slightly wounded, could do nothing to stop the getaway of the Daimler in which von Horssell had arrived. Further along the road the Daimler had been driven into a small party of men hurrying towards the 'Fisherman's Rest', and one man had been killed.

None of that surprised me, when I learned of it.

·　　·　　·　　·　　·

158

'What time is it?' I asked.

I had been conscious for some minutes. I felt nothing but a parched, burning sensation in the back of my throat, and a heavy headache. My eyes hurt, and I was glad that the only light in the room was a dim one, some way away from me.

I could just see someone at a table, near it, and when a chair scraped and he stood up I saw that it was Pinky. My own voice was cracked and hoarse: his was gruff.

' 'Lo, Bruce,' he said. 'Lucky young devil—nothing seems to kill you. Even von H. doesn't take his chance. How'd you feel?' His plump forefinger found my pulse, and he stared down at me with his head on one side, anxiety in his eyes. 'Not bad, not bad,' he observed. 'Can you talk?'

'Get me a drink,' said I. 'Tea or something that won't bite, please. Then I'll try.' I smoothed my forehead, and added with a touch of irritation: 'What time *is* it?'

'Half-past two,' he told me.

'Morning? The same morning?'

'If you mean that it's three hours or so since you went under, yes,' said Pinky, stepping to the door and pressing a bell. It was my room at the 'Fisherman's Rest', but Mary's bed was empty. 'Now don't ask a lot of foolish questions he went on sharply. 'Mary's all right—she got a worse dose than you, and von H. and the woman escaped. Did you learn anything?'

I started violently.

'Good God! He said tomorrow was the day of the invasion!'

'As soon as *that*!' The information shocked him badly, that was clear. 'We've got a few hours, even though his tomorrow is now today. What a blasted job this has been— snatches of information, nearly always too late.'

Dibble came in, with a tray of tea—a cup for Pinky

as well as myself. From that I judged that Pinky had been expecting me to come round for some time past, and he confirmed this. The doctor had assured him that it would be only a matter of hours, and that when I was awake I would have a considerable thirst.

As I drank, Pinky sent for Denyer.

That young man looked pale, but his eyes were bright —too bright and somewhat feverish I thought. He told me what I have already written, and Pinky kept nodding.

'You didn't hear them talk about anything happening tomorrow?' Pinky asked him.

'No,' said Denyer apologetically. 'I was unconscious most of the time, I'm afraid.'

'No need to be afraid of that,' growled Pinky. 'Now, I want you to pay particular attention. Rightly or wrongly, I think there is a lot in the fact that you saw Father André yesterday.'

'It was the day before yesterday now,' said Denyer stiffly. 'Of course there's something in it.'

'All right, all right,' said Pinky testily. 'We needn't go into that now. We *assume* you saw the *curé*, see? Start from there. Following me, Bruce?'

'No,' I said, looking up from my tea.

'Well now, here's the fact—the obvious fact. André is a priest. As such he was the only man at the refugee reception quay to hold frequent interviews with the refugees alone. Does that make sense?'

I started so much that I almost spilt my tea.

'By Jingo!' exclaimed Denyer. 'You've got something there!'

'Thank *you*,' said Pinky sardonically. 'Nice of you to say so. We work, then, on the assumption that Father André was operating for von H. He gave messages and instructions, and then from the camp the refugees went to all parts of the country. Neutral areas for the most part—

neutral!' sniffed Pinky. 'So, what is the obvious conclusion?'

Denyer said excitedly: 'Good heavens, sir, these Fifth Columnists are in all the refugee camps! I know I found a few, but I was dealing only with those who had paid a lot of attention to Fräulein Bruenning. The number who saw the *curé* are legend!'

'Exactly,' said Pinky, and a seraphic smile spread over his pink and plump countenance. 'However, it doesn't matter how many Nazis are with the refugees, it won't work. I've had every damned camp guarded as they've never been guarded before, and I've had a round-up of every billet in the country. Refugees as well as other aliens are all interned.'

'By George!' spluttered Denyer. 'It's a master stroke!'

'Oh, undoubtedly a master stroke,' conceded Pinky. 'I had a hell of a job to cut through red tape but this Government is not like the last, thank God. Well—if von H. hopes to do something tomorrow—today, all right, yes, *today!*—with the help of the refugees, he's unlucky.' Then with an abrupt change of tone and subject: 'Think you're all right on your pins, Bruce?'

'I'll try 'em,' I said.

One of the peculiar effects of the gas was that it was confined to the nose and throat and head, and apparently left the muscles of the body unaffected. I could walk freely. As soon as he realised this, Holt nodded to Denyer.

'All right, we'll see you in a few minutes. Stand by for action.'

'Right!' Denyer brought himself to attention, saluted, and clicked his heels. I saw a grin on Pinky's face as the door closed.

We waited until Denyer's footfalls had gone out of earshot, and then I tiptoed to the door, and opened it slowly.

No one was in sight.

I turned back to Pinky.

'*Well,*' he said, '*there's no doubt about that young swine, Bruce.* You knew it before, of course.'

I said: 'Yes, Pinky, I knew.'

And I knew also Pinky had been fooling for the past five minutes, and that my answers had the same object as his questions—to deceive young Mark Denyer. For we *knew* that he was working for von Horssell.

The problem was to turn that knowledge to account.

    •   •   •   •   •

The first really certain indication of Denyer's true position had come when he had mentioned Fräulein Bruenning. I knew that she had not been known as Bruenning at the quay: her name had been Dubois, or something similar. But Denyer had made a mistake perhaps without realising it when he had called her 'Bruenning'.

There were a dozen other indications.

I had first suspected it when Pinky had sent him down to the 'Fisherman's Rest' with that incredible story about the *curé*. Father André had died, of course—there was no doubt of that, and Pinky had confirmed it over the telephone; no kind of drug can induce a faked knife thrust to the heart. There was the camera, and the fact that Denyer had taken such convenient photographs. Far, far too convenient to be coincidence. When Pinky had 'phoned me at the 'Fisherman's Rest' I had talked in the belief that Denyer was listening in—and a few seconds afterwards I had seen him close to the door.

His boyish naiveté could so easily have blinded us, but Pinky had realised the truth after the Father André story, and sent him to me, thus setting the trap which had so nearly come off.

'Devil of it is,' growled Pinky, 'that I thought he'd get word to von H. that you were all going to be at Dent House, Guildford. I'd had the place surrounded with troops, and was all set to let von H. get through the cordon and then close in.'

'I guessed that when you told me to read the instructions out to the others,' I said. 'And I gave Denyer a chance of telephoning von H. He took it. I didn't listen in for fear he'd suspect. I wish to God I had!'

Pinky growled: 'Von H. was here, of course, that's why he decided to act before you got to Guildford. I thought that if there was one place he would keep away from after the bombing this would be it. Mistakes, mistakes, nothing but mistakes! The little swine sent the light up to guide the bomber, of course.'

'Pretending to keep in his room,' I growled. 'He had a dummy made under his bed to make it look as if he was taking cover there.'

There were other indications which had amounted to proof, and they flashed through my mind as I talked. Denyer had barged into my room when Mary had been there, and had apologised because he had 'forgotten' Mrs. Morely: he had known me for Murdoch and known that I was single: an odd lapse. But none of it was so important as the fact that Pinky's carefully prepared scheme to get von Horssell in the net had failed. We had put all our hopes in luring him to Dent House, Guildford.

'And now,' I said grimly, 'Denyer thinks we're feeling safe because we've got the refugee angle looked after. That's why he started the Father André hare.'

'Aimed to turn our attention into that channel,' Pinky said. 'Would have succeeded if we hadn't had him taped. However . . .' He glared at me. 'We've got him taped. What now?'

'Now,' I said, 'we pray that he contacts von H. again.'

21

Four on the Trail

It was useless for us to reproach ourselves: we had done more than might have been expected against von Horssell, for he had the weapon which the Nazis, in their years of careful and exhaustive preparation, made sure of getting —the initial advantage. They were lying in wait throughout the British Isles, thousands of Fifth Columnists ready on the order to rise and to do more damage to key points in Great Britain than had been done in Norway and Holland and Belgium. Oh, that was their plan, and I did not try to blind myself: nor did Pinky.

I opened my door, after the talk with Pinky. I half-expected to find Denyer within earshot, and my hand was at my pocket. However, Denyer was not in sight.

I slipped into the room where Mary was sleeping.

I looked down at her, seeing the slightly puffy nose and mouth and knowing that I looked very much the same. She was pale, but breathing easily and as if in natural sleep and not under the medico's sedative. I did not know whether I would live to see her again.

I had a peculiar feeling; not so much unreal as unnatural.

I turned slowly away from Mary, and in the passage outside I found Mick and Ted waiting. Pinky had gone.

'Percy's watching Denyer's room,' Ted said, 'from the outside.'

'Right. Take the front door, Ted, and you take the back, Michael. And pray as you've never prayed before that he makes a move.'

They moved off silently, while I returned to my room and put the telephone out of order. There was only one other in the 'Fisherman's Rest', and that was in a small closet just off the main hall. I found a comfortable seat on an old settle in full view of the stairs and the 'phone box.

There was a hush over the inn.

As I sat and waited I ran through what I had said to von Horssell, and the way Elsa had behaved suggested that I was not far from the truth.

I had suggested that the landing was to take place in this part of the country.

Sharp through the silence, I heard a door close.

After a pause there was a slow approach of footsteps towards the landing. I squeezed myself further back on the settle, but I could see the stairs clearly.

I saw a pair of rubber-soled shoes, and then the baggy flannel trousers of Mr. Mark Denyer.

He came down softly, making little noise, certainly none which would have awakened anyone sleeping. Next I saw his right hand, close to his side and holding an automatic.

He was half-prepared for trouble, and if it came to a point he meant to shoot his way out. My breathing was muted as I watched him come down. At the foot he looked about him, appeared satisfied, and walked to the front door.

The glass panels were broken, and had been boarded up. The door was locked, bolted and chained. With stealthy silence Denyer removed the chain. He was a bundle of nerves—more so even than I.

He opened the door and went out. Then I moved, hurrying to the back door. Just outside, Mick was waiting.

'The front,' I whispered.

We were wearing rubber-soled shoes, and made no sound as we hurried to join Ted. He was just ahead of us, a vague shadow against the darkness of the sky. Ahead, and walking towards the cliff road, was Denyer. Percy's shadow loomed up by my side, but he did not speak.

The road was steep, of course, and winding.

There was a narrow footpath leading to the top of the

cliff, and one which had been marked 'unsafe' because of the bombing. Denyer stuck to the road, Mick and I took the path. Soon we were high enough to be out of earshot, and for the first time since leaving the inn I spoke.

'If he seems to have a real chance of getting away, we shoot.'

'Right,' whispered Mick.

A moment later we reached the cliff road, and not far ahead of us was a small car, hidden from casual sight by bushes and trees. Mick took the wheel, and I waited by the running-board. The silence remained intense until it was broken by the sharp splutter of a motor-cycle engine on the road leading from the inn.

Mick started the car engine.

This car, and another on the other side of the downward road, was fitted with an engine as silent as they could be made. The splutter of the motor-cycle hid the sound that did come from it, and also that from Ted's.

The motor-cycle drew nearer.

'Our way,' I said, and Mick eased off the brakes so that the car was actually touching the road surface when the motor-cycle roared past. It was too dark to see clearly, but Denyer's flannel trousers made a faint, pale blur.

Mick accelerated.

Not far behind us was Ted Angell, and I knew that he would take a short cut across to the main Lynton Road, which was probably the one Denyer would take. As we went along, well within earshot of the motor-cycle, I was assessing the odds.

Three times in twenty miles Denyer was stopped by L.D.V. patrols. As many times we slowed down enough to show the special credentials that we carried, and continued the chase. Ted had rejoined us on the Lynton Road, and was no more than fifty yards behind us all the way.

Most of the time we kept track of Denyer only by the sound of his engine.

My jaws were sore because I so constantly gritted my teeth. A dozen times I thought we had lost him. When he took the Bath Road a little further on, it looked as if he were travelling towards London. By then it was nearly four o'clock, and soon it would be dawn.

We reached the outskirts of Knelton* about half-past four and again I expected to run straight through the High Street and get further along the Bath Road, but that did not happen. In the wide Market Square, which was sleeping under the light of the stars, and where there were only a few sandbags against the police station and the Town Hall, Denyer cut off his engine.

Mick slowed down at the approach to the Square.

We saw a policeman come from an A.R.P. post, and could hear the murmur of conversation. Then we were able to follow Denyer as he moved slowly towards the Town Hall.

Ted had also cut out his engine, and was alongside us.

'I'm going ahead,' I said. 'Fix it with that policeman.'

Percy Briggs fell in by my side and I cut across the Square to the big building to which Denyer had gone. I did not think then that we had come to the end of our journey. I did not know what had happened—and I had one thing only in mind.

I had to keep Denyer in sight.

He was at the front door of the building, the Town Hall. He stopped there, his finger on a bell. I was at the foot of the steps, and when the door opened I hurried up.

Denyer went in and did not close the door.

* There is of course no town or city of this name in the South of England. The assumed name is given for obvious reasons. No one except those directly involved were aware that at Knelton were the headquarters of the Nazi Fifth Column movement in Great Britain, nor that Public Utility Offices were being used by the Nazis. It is certain that no other Town Hall has been or is being used in this connection.—J.C.

I followed him, to find the big reception hall in darkness, and it was quite impossible for me to follow Denyer's movements. I heard a door squeak, and fancied that it was immediately ahead of me.

Percy bumped against my shoulder.

We went forward together, our eyes gradually becoming used to the light, and I saw the dark blotch of a door against the lighter colour of the walls. I sought and found the handle, turned it, and pushed the door open.

The room beyond was in complete darkness.

My heart was thumping, for I believe now that I had reached journey's end. I stopped, and whispered to Percy:

'Get back—telephone the County Headquarters where we are—the Chief is there.'

'Okay,' said Percy *sotto voce*.

He turned—and as he moved a light flashed on in the room where I was standing. As it flashed and I blinked, my hand dropped to my pocket. My gun was loaded, but I could not draw fast enough to do anything that night, for Denyer and two other men, neither of whom had I seen before, were by a door opposite. All three were armed.

'Don't move, *Mister* Murdoch,' said Denyer sharply. 'Nor you, Briggs.'

'You go to . . .' snarled Percy.

Perhaps he did not realise how much was at stake: perhaps he was quite careless of his own life when he felt that there was the need for action. At all events he leapt for the door, and doing so drew their fire.

For that split second none of them were looking my way, and I flashed my gun out and fired. Already their guns were barking. I heard Percy gasp, heard him crash to the floor.

Denyer and one of the others went down almost at the same time. The third man was still standing, but a lucky shot had sent his gun flying from his grasp. He backed away when I slewed my automatic towards him. The room,

168

a small one, reeked with smoke and the echoes of the shooting were still in my ears. I saw the door had closed automatically, and that there were no windows.

It was not likely that the shooting had been heard from outside.

The door by which the three men had stood was also closed.

I kept quite still, and for some seconds the only sound in the room was Percy's swearing. I dared not look towards him, although I knew that he was badly hurt. I said softly:

'Turn round.'

The man, a tall, young, blond man, hesitated and then obeyed. As he turned I moved, and I crashed the butt of my gun on the back of his neck.

I waited again.

Through the silence came Percy's voice:

'I'm—okay—Guv'nor.'

I glanced towards him, nodded and smiled.

I did not feel like smiling, for there was blood on the wooden floor of the room, blood from his wounds. His face was set, although he shook his head when I took a half-step towards him.

I wished Ted and Mick would hurry.

Mick did—but not in the way I wanted.

I heard the patter of rubber-soled shoes outside, and then he came into the room, pushing blindly against the door. There were other, heavier footsteps outside.

He banged the door to and leaned against it, white to the lips.

'The patrol's—outside—with von Horssell,' he snapped. 'Ted's out there.'

I said: 'Keep them away from here!'

I swung round towards the door which Denyer had been guarding. He was unconscious, as was the other man I had shot, and he whom I had clubbed. The door was not yet locked, and yet when I turned the handle and pushed, it refused at first to budge. I exerted greater pressure, and it opened an inch. I forced it wider, and squeezed through.

Mick was putting all his weight against the other door.

I went through, to find myself in a narrow, poorly lighted passage. The door which had been so heavy was padded and, I guessed, soundproof. Sound travelled in neither direction with the doors closed. The passage was no more than ten feet long, and a door at the far end was closed.

That opened more easily.

A brighter light met my eyes as I widened the gap, and I heard a voice which I had learned to hate so much: Elsa's. She was talking in German, and I gathered the drift and realised that she was talking into a radio-transmitter.

'*It is all ready, yes, all ready. Everything has been done, all arrangements are made . . . that is so, yes . . .*'

I had the door wide open, and stepped through.

She was sitting with her back towards me, and part of the wall opposite me was broken by the panelling of a radio-transmitter and a powerful receiving-set. She had headphones on, and I knew that she was talking with someone many miles away.

'*He is on the other transmitter, making final arrangements for the reception . . . Everything, I tell you, everything is ready. What? . . . They have started. Heil Hitler!*'

She moved a switch to disconnect, and for a moment sat back in her chair. I could not see her face, but her fair hair was dishevelled, and dropping to her shoulders. I could see the shoulders moving as she breathed with a fierce excitement. I crept towards her, making no sound, and I heard her mutter:

'*Today, it happens. Today.*'

'Well, well,' I said. 'We ought to celebrate.'

She swung round. I saw the shock and the fury in her eyes, but she was within a yard of me and of the gun which

pointed to her forehead. Her breast heaved as if she were
choking.

Then she snarled: *'You are too late, Murdoch. The
invasion has started!'*

22

'The Invasion Has Started'

I knew that no threat would make her submit to giving
information away. She was a blind follower of her Führer,
and whatever qualities she lacked she was loyal. To try to
make her give information would be a waste of time.

I said: 'So it's started, has it? That's too bad for your
Führer. Where's Baron von Horssell?'

Her eyes moved for a split-second towards a door opposite the one through which I had come. There were keys
on the small table next to the radio-transmitter.

'All right,' I said, 'I'll find him myself.'

'You . . .' she began.

She flew at me, ignoring the gun. I side-stepped, and as
she passed, I struck her on the back of the head, hard
enough to knock her out.

I prevented her from hitting the floor heavily. I slipped
a pair of handcuffs from my pocket, and clicked them over
her wrists. With a handkerchief I secured her slim ankles.
She was breathing very heavily, and I knew she would
be unconscious for some time.

I went back to Mick.

As I opened the door I heard the *crack!* of a shot. I saw
him sitting—yes, sitting!—in an easy chair, with a big
settee in front of him, protecting him from bullets coming
through the gap in the door leading to the reception hall.

He had dragged a heavy bookcase to the door, blocking it. He did not look up, but asked lightly:

'How're things with you?'

'Passable,' I said. 'Hold on.'

He nodded, and I went back.

I took the keys from the table and approached the door of the room where I should find von Horssell. The largest key of three fitted, and I pushed the door open slowly. Immediately I heard von Horssell's guttural tones. He talked quickly, with complete confidence, and what he said appalled me.

As I widened the gap, hearing that astonishing statement, I saw that he was sitting sideways to the door, and that behind him was another transmitter. Opposite him, and also sideways to the door, were two middle-aged men whom I had never seen before. When he paused, one man said tensely:

'You are quite sure nothing can go wrong?'

It was a mellow English voice, the voice of a man who might have held any position in England. I *hated* him. I could gladly have shot the three of them as they sat there.

'*Ach*, no,' said von Horssell. 'It has been done. I haff just had der vord of it. Also, der vord that der English working against me haff believed vot I vanted them to believe—that I am vorking through refugees. It iss not so. You need haff no fears, my friends. Knelton is der von place in all England vere der bombing vill never be. Der Führer will giff der orders. Even to der Führer I am too valuable for him to take der chances. From diss room in vich ve are sitting vill go der orders to all my men in England. You haff heard me giff instructions—you haff heard vot I say to you. Der attack has started.'

The second of the two men said tensely:

'Can you be quite sure we are safe?'

I saw the twist on the lips of the Withered Man—and I saw other things. He was sitting at a table, and in front of him was a hypodermic syringe. His forehead was beaded with sweat, and his face was the peculiar grey it had been when he had collapsed at Oxford. His breath was coming heavily.

'*Ja,*' he said. '*Ja*—all der things are cared for, haff no fear of that. Der town of Knelton is der first of der towns in England to be mine. You understand? Der visitors to der spa, to der healing vaters'—his teeth showed in gloating triumph—'for so long past, *dey* are agents for me. Der volunteers for der defence services—*dey* vork for me. In Knelton I haff two thousand men and vomen, all armed, all ready. Tonight, der police were raided and haff been replaced by my men.'

'It's colossal!' exclaimed one of that precious pair of Englishmen.

'Kolossal,' agreed von Horssell. '*Ja,* it iss all of dat. De other things, you understand them. It iss a town vich can be vell guarded from der inside, but it cannot vit' ease be attacked. Der hills are all about it. Der main roads are mined, and der rail lines also. Knelton is der operating centre for der attack from within!'

He stopped, and drew a deep, painful breath. I saw him glance towards the syringe.

'In two hours, after sunrise, all of der civilians in Knelton vill be told der town is under martial law, der law of der Führer. All resistance will be punished at vonce, vit' death. By sunrise, der aeroplanes vill begin to come, landing der troops and howitzers and other guns. Der centre of the country between der hills, guarded by der land mines I haff talked of, is goot for aeroplanes to land. From der centre it vill be able to bomb nearby towns an' ports, preventing reinforcements. Der part of England in vich you are now sitting belongs to der Fatherland. That iss understood?'

They looked *elated*.

I kept silent, for I wanted to hear every word I could.

173

I had a fleeting fear that Mick might not be able to hold out, but I pushed it aside.

Graham, too, would be doing the job Holt had given him.

That guttural voice droned on as the Withered Man described the size of the planned invasion and the cunning of it grew in gravity, in enormity. He broke off from time to time, and once his hand strayed to the syringe, but drew back. He told them everything, I believe because they were essential to his plans. They were the Quislings of Knelton, and of England.

He finished at last.

He leaned back in his chair, gasping, and again his fingers sought the syringe. He actually touched it when I fired.

The *crack!* of the shot must have dumbfounded them. The bullet struck the syringe and splintered it into pieces which flew into their faces. Even von Horssell covered his eyes. As the echo died down I went forward to the telephone.

Von Horssell was the first to recover.

'*Murd-och!*'

'As always,' said I, 'popping up at the inconvenient moment. Your drug won't be much good to you, will it?'

His face was working as he stared at the splintered remains of the syringe and the little pool of liquid which had spilled out on the table. He had to fight for his breath, as much from shock as from actual physical exhaustion.

I had once seen him collapse; and would again.

I lifted the telephone with my free hand. I could see all three, the faces of the two Englishmen far more frightened than von Horssell's. His pale eyes were pools of hatred, the square lips were turned back over his big teeth. His right hand was on the table, clenching and unclenching.

The operator answered; it was a man's voice.

'Number, please.'

'Sloane London 81812,' I said.

'Who is that speaking?' The voice grew sharp and suspicious, and then—only then—did I realise how far von Horssell had gone. For he laughed suddenly, a harsh laughter that was obscene, while the operator cleared the line swiftly.

The telephone exchange was in the hands of von Horssell's agent.

The shock of that realisation numbed me.

·   ·   ·   ·   ·

It is difficult even now to tell the whole truth about what happened during the night and early morning after the attack on the inn, the escape of von Horssell and Elsa, and the chase to Knelton.

I had made a vague guess at the way in which the invasion would start, and had not been far wrong. Choosing that night, since it was dark but not cloudy, the mass of the German air fleet came to England, but—it dropped no bombs.

That is one of the reasons why the news of the invasion did not leak out until long afterwards.

There was no apparent offensive, but high in the sky the horde of Nazi troop-carriers, parachute-carriers and tank-carrying 'planes came towards the coast. They flew so high that many of them came through undetected, but the chief cunning of the manœuvre was the fact that in *ninety* places on the coast fighter-machines and light bombers came over, and attracted the fire of the A.A. defences and the onslaught of the Home Defence fighters. While nearly a hundred battles were being waged in what was believed to be a preliminary to the biggest bombing onslaught on Great Britain yet conceived, the monster 'planes came from the south-west, west and north-west. None of the normal routes was used by those leviathans of the skies as they made their way at five miles a minute towards the comparatively undefended west of England and Scotland. They landed within twenty miles of Land's End, and within five miles of Cape Wrath in the extreme north. Their parachutists descended like butterflies. But . . .

They started no offensive.

Light tanks were landed from planes in outlying places, and camouflaged so that it was impossible to see them. The success of the whole operation depended on one thing only—the complete paralysing of the L.D.V. corps in the areas where the invaders were landing. That was done with the same cunning as the sending over of the fighters to take care of the Coastal Command machines. A few parachutists landed within plain sight in the most conspicuous places in the west country and the whole of the western coastline. Without knowing that these troops were not the real suicide squad of the Nazis, the L.D.V. attacked with vigour and success, and the Press next morning told of the complete rounding-up of the parachute troops. As far as it was known, that was true. But the great mass of the 'chutists, with transparent parachutes and wearing dark clothes so that they were virtually invisible, landed without being discovered. *They did not bring arms.*

Arms in profusion were waiting at the points which von Horssell had prepared beforehand. The plan was sublime in its audacity. The invading force, some thirty thousand men, was to be in the country for at least twenty-four hours, and perhaps longer, before the air invasion proper started, with heavy bombing. Coincidental with that attack would be vast acts of sabotage, directed chiefly towards electric power stations, waterworks and lines of communication.

I had no doubt that von Horssell had this worked out to the last degree; that every town, village and city had its nucleus of Fifth Columnists. In some centres, as in Knelton, he was so strongly entrenched that he could take control in a matter of hours.

Knelton, with its surrounding hills and its own flat valley, was the ideal spot for the headquarters. Unless it could be raided without loss of time von Horssell would have control so strong that it would be difficult to take. From it he would send out his radio orders to other centres; from it German bombers would mass to the attack on towns and cities which were considered undefended.

If the plans worked, the attack would pulverise the south and south-west country until everything was paralysed.

And the telephone exchange was already manned by his men.

I had forgotten the two Quislings, who had withdrawn to a corner, as if frightened of their lives. Only von Horssell showed no fear. Instead there was that look of gloating triumph, as if he knew that I was acknowledging defeat.

I looked at the radio-transmitter.

I could not operate it: of the four who had come on this desperate trail only Percy could, and he—I thought—was probably bleeding to death not fifty feet away. I was wrong about Percy, and von Horssell first told me that, although unwittingly. He looked from me to the door, and automatically I stepped to one side.

The door opened slowly.

It was Percy, crawling on his hands and knees. He butted the door open with his head. There was blood matting his waistcoat, and a deep gash in his right cheek, but he looked up at me with a grin in his eyes.

'Okay,' he said, 'I thought you'd need me.'

23

S.O.S.

Von Horssell made a final effort then.

I could see that he was close to collapse. He had stayed without his dope until the last minute, and now had no chance of exerting a furious burst of energy. He lunged forward, however, with his sword stick snatched from a resting-place close by him.

I fired.

I struck the handle of the stick, and shot the top joint off his forefinger: I saw that clearly. He snatched his hand away and bellowed, more in rage than with pain. The stick dropped, the point of the sword quivering in the parquet floor.

Von Horssell dropped into his chair, blood streaming from his hand and his face ashen grey.

'Percy,' I said very softly. 'Get a wavelength that will reach London. Tell them that Knelton must be surrounded by strong forces. Tell them thousands of Germans have taken the city.'

'*Gawd!*' gasped Percy. He had reached the chair in front of the transmitter, and was dragging himself up.

'Tell them that an invasion is now on,' I said. 'That aeroplanes and troop-carriers can be expected at Knelton within an hour, and fighters must be here to stop them landing. Got that?'

Percy gasped, sweat streaming down his face.

'Okay, I've got it.'

'Right,' I said. 'Right.' As he fiddled with the instrument I added: 'Is Mick all right?'

'Still holding 'em off.'

'Fine,' said I, and then my voice hardened. 'You two, get over by the door.'

The two renegades did not argue, while I watched them as well as von Horssell. I judged that he had only minutes of consciousness left, and indeed he collapsed suddenly. I did not take chances, however, but took off my tie and bound his hands, although his gross body was like a log.

'Through that door,' I ordered the others.

They went out like whipped curs.

I urged them into the room which Mick was holding. Mick still sat in the chair, but there was a strained expression on his face and a litter of empty cartridge cases by him. As we went into the room a burst of fire splintered the back of the settee, which he had pushed a little to one side.

'We haven't much time,' said Mick, without glancing round. 'Have you done anything?'

'Percy's trying to now,' I said. 'Take this.'

'This' was my spare gun. I had still a bullet or two in the other, enough for the Quislings who cowered back against the wall.

'Thanks,' said Mick, mechanically.

'And now, gentlemen,' I said in a voice which made the pair jump, 'what other way is there out of this place?'

The shorter of the two men licked his lips. He was a plump, benevolent-looking fellow, with a fringe of grey hair, but his mouth was loose and slobbery.

'Th-there . . .' he started.

'Shut up, Cassel!' snapped the taller of the couple. 'They can't get through, and there are hundreds of the Baron's men coming.'

I shot him through the chest, high up.

I did not want to kill him, for he would be needed for questioning when all this was over. He gasped, and staggered back against the wall, a hand at his chest. When he took it away he saw the blood and gave a high-pitched, unnatural

179

scream, then slowly collapsed. I had seen too many refugees machine-gunned to be sorry for him, and I rasped to Cassel:

'Do you want the same?'

'Oh, my God, no!' gasped Cassel. 'Through—through the Baron's room, there's a way out to the roof! The other door's been blocked up, you can only get out through the roof.'

'Go ahead and show me how,' I ordered.

He turned without any argument, but he could hardly put one leg before the other, he was so frightened. Altogether, I had been out of von Horssell's room for seven or eight minutes. When I went into the room next to Mick's I saw Elsa still stretched out, unconscious, and I expected to find von Horssell there too.

I did not: the man had gone!

    •   •   •   •   •

It was easy enough to understand.

I did not think so then: I was stupefied to find him missing, and my head reeled. I saw Percy sprawled across the radio-transmitter, his head pillowed in his hands, and then a shot came from the ceiling, fired through a hole which I had not seen. I ducked, instinctively, and the bullet missed. Cassel gasped and turned round: turning, he put himself between me and a second bullet. It struck him in the forehead, and he did not live to cry out again.

I found cover by the door, and fired upwards.

I hit someone, for I heard a gasp, but when I pulled the trigger again there was a *click!* and I had lost my second chance. A split-second later a dull bang came from the ceiling, and the trap door there closed down.

I did not know whether Percy had got his message out.

I stepped to him, sweating, hot, and yet with an icy fear

at the back of my mind. I saw the ugly bruise on the back of his head and obviously he had been struck from behind by someone who had come through that trap-door. I looked up at it helplessly, realising that there must be some kind of a loft-ladder or a telescopic staircase, but that there was little hope of operating it, and even if I succeeded I had no weapon.

Then I found new hope.

I patted Percy's pocket, and found a gun. I examined it quickly, finding that it was nearly fully loaded. By then I was in the room with Mick. The stutter of the machine-gun had stopped.

'Stick to it,' I urged. 'And you . . .'

I swung round to the wounded man, who had not lost consciousness. He flinched: I think he thought I would shoot him again. I roared, much louder than I intended:

'The switch for the staircase—where is it?'

He gave in without a fight at all.

'Ab—above the radio.'

I rushed back to the room from which von Horssell had disappeared. I had no idea of the position outside, but guessed a large-scale attack was on the way. Von Horssell's preparations, making only one way of entry to the radio-transmitting rooms, rebounded to my advantage.

I found a small lever above the apparatus.

I pulled it, and in front of my eyes the hole appeared in the ceiling. There was no ladder, after all, but a small platform with a railing running about it. It was easy to see how von Horssell had been taken up, and I actually saw a smear of blood on the platform as I stepped on it. It was operated electrically, of course, and the control switch was set in one of the rails.

As the lift crawled towards the hole in the ceiling, I waited with my gun ready, but fearful of an attack from above. My head was on a level with the ceiling at last, however, and there was no attack. The room above was in darkness, and I searched for a switch as I passed through the hole and found one on the right side. Bright electric light showed me that I was in an office large enough for half a dozen people.

It was empty.

But a door stood ajar at the far end, and through that I could hear the sound of movement. When I reached the door, I found that it led to a narrow stone staircase, down which sound was travelling and echoing cavernously, making the source of it sound much nearer than it was.

I mounted swiftly.

At the first landing it became spiral in shape, and progress was slow. I could hear voices, and the deep hum of an engine. why I assumed that it was some kind of plant I hardly know. I reached the top of the spiral, and felt the coolness of the night air. In a few seconds I was on the flat roof of the Knelton Town Hall, with the stars above me dimmed in the first grey light of dawn.

I saw the gyroplane then.

It was some thirty yards away from me, already off the roof and hovering in mid-air. I could see three or four faces against the cockpit window, and I saw that the door was open. As I watched I realised why they had waited, and I flung myself face downwards, hugging the wall of a chimney stack close by.

The bomb dropped within twenty yards of me.

Had it been ten yards nearer I would never have had a chance. As it was the gust of wind from the explosion lifted me bodily, and then threw me against the wall. I felt as if every bone in my body was breaking, and had to gasp painfully for breath.

In my ears was the droning of the gyroplane's engine, and I could see it some thousand feet above me. For the first time I began to wonder why von Horssell had been taken from the building although it was surrounded—according to him—by his own men, and the town was in his hands.

I understood soon afterwards.

Three or four incendiary bombs were burning furiously on the roof, and as I watched the machine going upwards one burst, sending its little satellites about the roof. My coat caught fire and I beat it out against the wall before going to the edge of the roof.

I could see down into the Market Square.

I could see the sandbagged entrance of the police station opposite the Town Hall, and two or three other posts, manned with machine-guns. The guns were in action, although they fired with little or no noise—another Nazi refinement to make the surprise of an attack more complete.

But—why in action?

I understood a moment or two later, for I saw the first of the parachute troops landing!

I had seen the confusion behind the lines of Holland and Belgium, but I had never been so confused as I was myself then. For the men coming down were dressed in English uniforms, and some were actually firing as they dropped. There were thirty or forty of them, and high in the sky I could see the 'planes from which they had come.

I discerned the red, white and blue roundels of the R.A.F.

Were these men English? Or were they Germans in disguise?

Who were the men manning the machine-gun posts in the Market Square?

There seemed no way of making sure, but one offered itself. I kept behind the parapet of the roof, taking no chances. Quite suddenly I saw a man I recognised behind one machine-gun embankment.

It was Meltze!

So von Horssell had not lied: he had taken possession of the key points of Knelton.

I fired, and Meltze staggered from the gun, his hands clasping his chest. Another man took his place and I missed him with two shots, then caused only a slight wound with the third. He carried on. They were clearly convinced that help would come soon, for they were fighting with complete confidence down in the square. One or two, recovering swiftly, had landed and were taking cover behind small buildings and in doorways while they fitted their machine-guns together.

I fired again, and scored a hit; but it was my last bullet.

Then a *thump* came close behind me, and as I turned abruptly I saw a man in khaki. He lost his balance but I grabbed at him: he would have gone over the edge of the building but for that.

'Ta,' he said as he staggered up, and then he began to unstrap himself quickly. 'We'll soon clean up that mob.'

He continued to smile—and to work.

He had his gun in position within minutes, and then he rained a stream of lead down on the Fifth Column below. One after another threw up his hands and collapsed, and I could see the red blood that streamed on the cobbles. Men came hurrying from the police station to replace the injured, but the man at my side had remarkable accuracy.

Other parachutists were operating from doorways and corners, and I saw them advancing on the police station *and* on the Town Hall, part of which was obviously held by the Fifth Columnists.

'I'm going down,' I said to the parachutist, and he nodded while keeping up the deafening stutter of his fire. I reached the spiral staircase, rushing across one patch of the roof where the fire had caught and was blazing furiously. I needed a stirrup-pump to put out those flames.

Then I looked into the top chamber of the staircase and saw smoke and flame billowing upwards. That was the

moment when I knew why they had rushed von Horssell
away. There had been a timed fire-bomb inside the building, and it had gone off.

24

Temporary Finish

I hesitated, with the smoke coming more furiously about
me, and the heat of the flames close to my face. I wondered
if there was a chance of getting down, and why the place
had been set on fire.

To destroy records, of course.

There might be a dozen more bombs down below, explosive as well as incendiary, but it was clear that I must
try to stop that fire getting a hold. I turned to call the parachutist, but he was at my side, and his stirrup pump, a part
of the general equipment, was in his hands.

'Blimey!' he exclaimed.

I was reminded vividly of Percy by that ugly, smiling
suicide squadman as he pushed his way past me and started
squirting the pump, filled not with water but a chemical.
The first rush of flames died down almost at once.

'Take one of these,' said the parachutist.

He handed me an asbestos glove, and with it on my
left hand I could move. The iron metal rail was red hot,
and I could feel the heat through the crêpe of my shoes,
and smell the pungent odour of burning rubber. As we
reached the end of the spiral and neared the stone staircase, flames and smoke billowed ahead of us, making us
choke and gasp.

He played the extinguisher, and the flames died down.

I was choking and gasping for breath, but it seemed as if we were getting on top of the fire. He exclaimed suddenly, and I saw the hose and fire-hydrant curled on the wall near the head of the staircase. We unlimbered it and went downstairs, to the room which contained the lift.

This was filled with a heavy cloud of smoke, but did not seem to be burning.

It was my turn to go first, since we used the lift and I could operate it. Percy was still curled over the radiotransmitter. He had sent his message through, of course—the 'chutist was part of the answer.

The smoke was not so thick here.

Mick, still in the ante-room, but no longer in his chair, swung round when he heard us. I saw the 'chutist move his machine-gun upwards, and I pushed it aside.

'Not him!' I rapped.

'Well, well, well,' Mick said, his voice refreshingly casual. 'What have you brought me, Santa Claus?' He grew serious. 'There's a bunch holding the front hall against an attack. Can you fix 'em, Alfred?'

'Okay,' said 'Alfred'.

He had no illusions, that young soldier. He poked the nose of the machine-gun through the door, and sprayed the backs of the Fifth Columnists holding the entrance to the Town Hall. Four went down: the others swung round, giving up their fight and thrusting their hands upwards.

'Alfred' sniffed.

'You oughta git all I can give yer,' he said with feeling.

There was a brief interval before a Tommy came cautiously up the steps leading to the reception hall. He was carrying a Bren gun, but had a sudden burst of firing greeted him he would have had no chance at all. Instead he saw Mick and 'Alfred' and me, and a cheery grin crossed a Cockney face.

'Wotcher, blokes,' he said. 'Fahnd a back way in then? Okey-doke, what abaht puttin' that fire aht?'

A platoon of men followed him, and the Town Hall was occupied within five minutes. By then the shooting had stopped in the Market Square, and infantry who had ridden into the town in lorries were going from house to house. A few frightened women were at their front doors, but far more who seemed no more frightened than the parachutist were already bringing cups of tea to their doors, and others bottles of beer.

There was a *festive* air about Knelton.

It seemed absurd, but it was so.

That hour of shooting might have brought a greater tragedy than had ever befallen the people of the country: and within ten minutes of its stopping the streets were crowded, and there was laughter and rough jokes.

I could not believe it was really over.

From von Horssell's grim monologue I had expected something far more desperate, but I had not allowed for the attack preceding von Horssell's plans by an hour or more.

I had a long telephone talk with Pinky.

Graham, who had left us on his secret mission, had gone to the seaplane which had been intended to take us to Guildford, and had flown it at a high altitude, *following the course of Ted's car and mine*. The roofs of both saloons had been covered with a specially devised phosphorous paint, enabling them to be seen from the air. Graham, then, had seen us stop at Knelton, and had radioed the Pink 'Un, who had gone on to Bristol where he maintained a branch office.

Percy's S.O.S. had reached London and had been relayed to Bristol.

Graham's message had inspired the Pink 'Un to get troops and carrier 'planes ready: Percy's had been the signal for action. The speed of the counter-attack coupled with the fact that von Horssell had been out of action had pulled off a complete surprise. None of the Fifth Column's plans had been put into action, but the party which had taken control of the police station and other key points had believed there would be help from the air at any moment, and had kept fighting.

The help had not come because von Horssell had never sent his message.

'No doubt about that,' Pinky said into the telephone. I told him what had happened my end, of course, and he never needed to be told a thing twice. 'Caught him on the hop, after all, and Denyer led us to him.'

'*Us*,' I said.

'Don't be insolent!' rapped Pinky, but I could imagine the beam on his chubby face. 'Damned good work, Bruce. I've given the word to Whitehall, of course. It's not all over yet, but I don't think it will be long.'

I was given a bed in the best hotel, and slept uninterruptedly for eight hours. Before then I had seen Percy and Ted into hospital—Ted had a head wound, but was conscious—and had made arrangements with Mick also to get a night's rest; or what remained of that night.

Many things happened while I slept.

Pinky, for instance, came to Knelton, with several of his office staff, and they went through the papers at the Town Hall one by one. They found the complete plans of the points for landings, and the small villages and farmhouses, controlled by Nazi agents.

There were, as I have said, thirty thousand Nazi soldiers, desperate men of the suicide brigade, in Great Britain. They did not remain free for twelve hours. The fact that they had come without arms, which were to have been distributed by von Horssell, or at his orders, had made the round-up easier.

All this was nearly over when I woke up, and, after a bath and a shave, went over to the Town Hall. Pinky was installed in von Horssell's office, and he looked up perkily.

' 'Lo, Bruce. Well, here we are then. We got the gentleman.'

I frowned: 'We stopped him, but he's missing.'

'Same thing,' said Pinky airily, although both of us knew that it was not. He told me what was happening, then stabbed his podgy forefinger towards me. 'It was big, Bruce, a fine conception. Thank God it failed!'

'Yes,' I said grimly. 'But how did he get control of the places?'

Pinky sat back, cocked his head on one side, and then said gently:

'Don't tell me you haven't guessed *that*!'

'I haven't,' I admitted.

'Simple,' said Pinky, 'the simplest thing you know. He had forged Government orders for the commandeering of all the places, and put them into operation yesterday afternoon. There was no time for argument. People were told—apparently officially—to billet as many soldiers as they could. The villagers all say they thought they were billeting our troops.'

'Good God!' I exclaimed. 'And, Pinky—the organiser got away.'

'Don't call me Pinky,' said the Pink 'Un testily.

'No, sir.'

'And that's worse,' snapped Pinky, but he rubbed his hands and beamed. 'He made only one mistake, really—one big one. He relied on Denyer getting away with too much.'

'That boy scout might have tricked us,' I said, 'but I can't see why he told us the truth about von Horssell.' That question had puzzled me, although I had formed a theory which I imagined fitted the facts. Pinky confirmed it.

'The Teuton's inbred mistake—over-confidence. There had been rumours of a Withered Man. Von Horssell took a chance of confirming it and putting a man into a position with me where he would help to look for his master. But von Horssell overlooked the possibility that we would rumble it. Yet he let his man carry on.'

It is hard not to admire Pinky, but he does always look so indecently pleased with himself when he's on a winner.

'All right,' I said drily. 'It took you quite a time to rumble him, though.'

'Don't you believe it,' said Pinky vigorously. 'I knew it from the start, but I didn't have early information about the woman. Poor André,' added Pinky, and meant it.

I stared.

'What are you getting at?'

'Father André,' said Pinky gently, 'was one of us. Looking for the Withered Man. *And* he had some information, that is why he was killed. And don't ask me why I didn't tell you,' went on the Pink 'Un sharply. 'You had to be pretty convincing to Denyer, and you were.'

I leaned forward and gripped the Pink 'Un's shoulder.

'Pinky,' I said, 'I hand it to you. I thought von Horssell had the most warped mind in the Intelligence Service. I was wrong—freely I admit that I was wrong.'

And that, of course, made Pinky crow with delight.

.   .   .   .   .

It was really over.

Denyer had been killed, probably by my bullet, and there were none of the Fifth Columnists listed in the records at Knelton who remained free after that day. The arrests were on so large a scale that no effort was made to report it by radio or by the Press: all that was officially said was that detention of Fifth Columnists on a large scale had been carried out simultaneously in all parts of the country.

I thought that Elsa should have been tried forthwith and shot but it is impossible to understand completely the British temperament. She was imprisoned, and when

—a week after the clear-up—I next saw Mary, Elsa still awaited trial.

Mary had been sent to London, and I had stayed down in the West Country, helping to clear up. Mick stayed with me. Percy was lucky, thank God—although it would be months before he was on his feet. Ted was even luckier.

At my flat in Park Lane, on our own, and with a note from Pinky telling us that if we wanted that week's leave we could have it, Mary said:

'There's only one thing wrong, Bruce.'

'Yes,' I said, 'the Withered Man's alive. But we'll get him one day.'

'Do you know,' said Mary, 'it wouldn't surprise me if you *wanted* another go at him.'

I put a hand beneath her chin, and said:

'I want to make use of that marriage licence, sweet, and then to have a week in Dorset where we can honeymoon without interruption, and forget von Horssell and Pinky and the whole damned shoot of them.'

'Carried unanimously,' said Mary.

We used the licence: we went to Dorset: but we did not forget. I knew I would never get the Withered Man out of my mind while he continued to live.

But that didn't stop Mary and me from enjoying life, nor Pinky from making plans. And ten days afterwards he sent for us, and when we had settled in the office, glared and said:

'Now listen, you two. You *ought* to know as much about Fifth Columnists as anyone in the country.'

'Granted,' I said amiably.

'There surely isn't *another* scare,' Mary said, and I knew she was seeing von Horssell in her mind's eye.

'Scare?' said Pinky. 'What scare? Of course there isn't, I don't think we'll have much trouble over here, except in isolated instances.'

'Oh,' said Mary. Her eyes gleamed, and her voice was so mild that Pinky did not get it immediately. 'What do you want us to do, write a book about it?'

'It?' said Pinky. 'What do you mean, it?'

'The Fifth Column,' said Mary.

'Don't be so insolent!' roared Pinky. 'Write a book be damned! But you've studied their methods, and we could use a Fifth Column in Germany. Any bright ideas?'